PRAISE FOR, FOR THE LOVE OF DOG TALES

"It was so incredibly moving and truly gives a voice to dogs living at the mercy of a world not of their making."

Heather Allen
President & CEO
HALO Animal Rescue

"Thank you for a book that not only gives a voice to our canine friends and their struggles but also compels us to raise our voices to end that struggle."

Top Dog Eileen Proctor
Pet Lifestyle Expert and Animal Welfare Advocate

"You have captured in this work something greater than just a "dog's tale". Your story speaks to the greater issue of man's inhumanity to man as well as all living creatures."

Valerie Fair
Artist

Musette El-Mohammed

For the Love of Dog Tales

"Life's Story" told through the experiences
of our closest companion.

I L Cannon

Thanks for your contribution to making a life
long dream come true!

Irvin L. Cannon

Acknowledgments

After a little over fifteen years of gathering dust, this book has now become a reality.

I would first like to thank my son, Irvin Jr., who not only inspired me to write these stories, but who also stood by his dad believing in him—even when I failed.

To Mom and Dad, I wish to all heaven that you both still walked this earth. I miss your presence, I miss your touch, and I thank you for cultivating my imagination and wonder throughout all of my life.

To my loving sisters, Yvonne and Angela, I can honestly say *I don't think I would still be alive without you.*

To my remarkable, loving wife, Dubby, it was solely you who got this whole ball rolling after all these years. You actually believed in me, motivated me, and most importantly, loved this lowly creature. Thank you.

For their creative contributions to this book's creation, thanks to Valerie, Kevin, Timothy Sr., Tweety, and all my "Pork-N-Bean Head" nephews and nieces.

And finally to my daughter, Taylor, thanks for the motivation that keeps me going in hopes of you one day reuniting with your brother and me.

Dedication

This book is dedicated to the Memory of my parents Kathleen and Robert Cannon, to the memory of two true heroes, D. Daniels (Detroit Police Department) and J. Bird (Denver Police Department). And in special memory of my own Angel, Angela my Baby Sister. One of my biggest supporters, who passed just before this publication. We love and miss you Angel.

CONTENTS

Introduction

Who could forget the old-time favorites such as *Lassie*, *The Littlest Hobo*, and *Rin Tin Tin*? And oh, what fond memories they bring of childhood! Back then it was absolutely every growing child's fantasy to own a faithful collie like Lassie or a courageous German shepherd like Rin Tin Tin to always protect him or her from ever-lurking evil.

Dogs are considered to be one of the top three household pets. More than likely, it was an initial contact with a canine that introduced most people to their first link to the animal kingdom. Honestly, what warms the heart and stirs the emotions more than those four-legged, furry, cuddly friends known as canines? They are as close as any family member—always by your side, never yielding, a source of unconditional love and devotion. Yet, however integral dogs are to our lives, their world, though ultimately framed by us, is a mystery.

Let's now journey through time with a tiny inquisitive angel and travel back to the 1980s to bear witness to a different world: the world through a canine's eyes. My hope is that these stories, like stories of old, prove timeless, haunting, humorous, tragic, and lovable.

Prologue

Amid the heavenly aura and illuminating starlight, the Lord is speaking as we use our gifts of discernment to listen to the sound of a woman's voice, the voice of God, filtering through the clouds. "And who's to say that of my creatures who are always scampering from the many obstacles placed in their way of survival—" We witness the Lord effortlessly display panoramic views of animals throughout existence. The first reveals the precious ant running desperately underfoot, attempting to avoid being crushed in a busy intersection, "—time and again. Yet to some, the very lives of these creatures are next to nonexistent; people do not spare a thought as to what they may casually trample underfoot or hurt during their mass productions to satisfy man's often selfish hunger for entertainment and advancement."

"The creatures have proven themselves, Lord," a childlike, angelic voice calls out.

"Yes. It would prove surprising to humans that all of my smaller creatures are not without a soul."

"Hear, hear!"

"And now that brings me to one of my most joyous creations—"

"Oh?" The comment stimulating his interest, the tiny angel named Brian materializes in a twinkling mist.

"—the embodiment of unselfish dedication and loving devotion towards its master with little to nothing expected in return."

Brian says, "Why Lord, how thoughtful. I—"

The Lord chuckles. "Oh Brian, I'm not describing you."

"Oh! Ahem. Sorry. Ah, will You continue?"

"For man, these creatures warm the heart from the time that they're born and become the most faithful of companions until the moment I call them home. This species was initially created wild—not unlike all my creatures—but through the course of time mankind, even through my disapproval, was able to domesticate a few."

"You truly are the forgiving Spirit."

"Now, unlike their wild cousins living on the outskirts of human civilization, these creatures are welcomed to flourish with people, living side-by-side with them. This arrangement is mostly for the better, but sometimes it's for the worst."

Brian, confused, asks, "Lord, I'm at a loss here, although I do have an idea…"

The Lord chuckles mildly and says, "Oh, my dear Brian, I shall cease keeping one of my most trusting angels in suspense."

Brian, feeling honored, says, "Well, I—"

"Brian, I'm discussing one of my creatures whose name given to it by humans contradicts the entire essence of its breeding. The very word has become a negative in human languages when the creature is actually a positive in people's lives. Indeed, Brian, I'm talking about the dog—the canine, man's best friend."

"Why of course, my Lord, and might I say one of your better creations indeed!"

"Yes," the Lord sighs, "in light of all things, one of my premiere creations. However, people are not always kind to man's best friend, with their preoccupation to conquer and destroy, leaving in their wake war, starvation, prejudice, crime, homelessness, hatred, and so on."

Suddenly, there is an explosion of thunder and the crackle of lightning in the background. Brian hastens to speak. "A little more patience, oh Lord. We are yet children."

"Accurate and well-spoken, my compassionate angel. You have in the past stood so bravely in man's defense, being yet a mere child when you accepted my calling."

"It's true, Lord," Brian replies, suddenly feeling hollow inside. The angel lifts his head as he feels some light stardust grace his shoulder, revealing an illuminated vision of his parents, distant and Earthbound.

"Children are invaluable; with hearts so pure, they share a common likeness with canines. It's of my own design that they share a special affinity."

Brian, holding a small, tattered teddy bear in one hand, sits on a stoop, looking up inquisitively. "Lord, I'm afraid I don't understand."

"Brian, I'm merely saying there is nothing more extraordinary than the relationship between a child and a dog. Here, let's look at the lives of just a few of my canine champions."

The Lord's glow gives way to galaxies, the galaxies to constellations, the constellations to stars, the stars to a familiar moon, and finally, to Earth.

Brisk

It was nightfall, and inside a large metropolis sat a young boy nicknamed Tidbit, clad in his brother's baggy hand-me-down clothes. He was sitting in a storage room in the rear of a bar, working diligently rearranging boxes. Times were difficult—it was hard for a man to feed an entire family—and Tidbit's family was barely surviving. Therefore, everyone had to pull his or her weight to make do. Tidbit considered himself lucky to have an odd job such as this. The money earned went toward his school lunch and the small savings he kept to build toward his dream of being able to one day attend college. The cleaning job he didn't mind, for it helped to feed him and his family. However, he detested what was now going on down in the basement.

Below were the kennels that held the fighting dogs, and inside the makeshift ring two competitors fought, surrounded by loud, jubilant, drunk, betting spectators. As the two dogs tore into each other—much to the heartened delights of the men surrounding the combatants—another set of captive eyes watched from a distance away, inside the kennels.

Brisk, an American Staffordshire terrier—otherwise known as a pit bull—stood attentive in his kennel, occasionally barking, then feinting and ducking side-to-side, observing the competitors closely. "Watch it, Needlenose! Boy, that young kid got some good stuff on him."

Worm, an aging boxer and fellow competitor who'd been bested by Brisk a number of times—but like a true sportsman still considered Brisk his closest associate—yelled, "He does, but he's still young yet. He needs to learn the ins and outs of the fight game!"

Within moments, the fight was over as Needlenose, with dominant vigor, pinned the younger dog to the ground, its tail firmly planted between its legs in submission. Two men separated them, and one of the men wiped Needlenose off with a towel, returning him to his cage alongside Brisk.

"Good fight there," Brisk said. "Way ta stick 'im."

"Thanks, thanks," Needlenose panted. "You think maybe I shoulda led stronger toward the right?"

Worm, speaking with confidence, said, "You handled the young lad just fine. Not too rough, not too soft. Good stuff there!"

Almost immediately, two more gladiators were called into the smoke-filled, closed-circle coliseum lit by a solitary lamp. One of the handlers picked up Brisk as another handler reached into the opposite kennel.

"Show that youngster a few tricks now," Worm cheered. "Get 'im, Brisk!" Needlenose also shouted his approval.

The handlers held the dogs in the center of the ring for the face-off. Both dogs snarled, baring teeth with menacing intent.

"The name's Chip, old timer. No hard feelings after I trounce you."

"I go by the name Brisk, pup. Nice meeting you. Keep your guard up and let's give 'em a good show." The handlers let them go, and the two dogs boldly jousted about the ring.

After a few moments, Brisk, being favored and getting the better of the pup, encouraged his younger opponent. "Good stamina, Chip. I bested you this time, but in a few short weeks, you're gonna make a fine competitor!" Brisk gave Chip, who stood with his head lowered, a mild head butt of confidence.

As fight night drew to a close, the handlers fed the dogs in the kennels.

Worm, the first to notice their visitor, lifted his head from his dish. "I say, Brisk, looks like that lad who's taken a fancy to you has popped in again."

"So he has!" Brisk looked up from his bowl, displaying his eagerness by wagging his tail.

Needlenose, munching from inside his bowl, grunted, "I wonder what the kid sees in 'im."

Tidbit opened Brisk's cage, held the dog in his hands, and did a careful inspection. All the while, Brisk showered his face with licks.

"Not too much damage tonight. That's good. That's the way I like my dog. And soon as I can afford you, you are going to come home and live with me and my two brothers and sister!"

From upstairs, Tony, the bar's owner, hollered down, "Tidbit, haul yer butt from down there now so I can pay ya and you scoot home!"

Tidbit gave "his dog" another hug then placed him back into the kennel. All the dogs watched him climb up the stairs.

At the top of the stairs standing guard was Buzzsaw, angry on his leash and growling, snarling, and threatening anyone in his presence. He was a huge 160-pound Rottweiler, every ounce of his body fierce. He was the guard dog of the bar, and for obvious reasons, none of the other dogs cared for his hostile demeanor.

Buzzsaw angrily charged at Tidbit while the dogs in the kennel gasped. Tidbit hesitated to go around him, but Buzzsaw's chain snapped to its limit. The dogs in the kennel barked their protests at Buzzsaw as Tidbit ran safely around him.

"Buzzsaw, you're a jerk!"

"The kid isn't a threat to you!"

"Lighten up, you moron."

"You're not so tough!"

"Shad up, all of yous!" Buzzsaw yelled back. "Keep on yapping and I'll bust my chain, come down there, and eat you all like canned sardines!"

The dogs' protests simmered down, none of them really wanting to provoke Buzzsaw, who in most dogs' minds could do what he'd threatened.

"Oh, he's not so tough. Ole Worm over there whipped him once," one of the dogs said, trying to instill some bravery. But Worm was quick to interject, "Ah. That, my boy, was a long, long time ago when he was but a pup and I was much, much younger."

"Ah, Worm, that don't mean nothing," Needlenose said, still protesting. "We still ought to all jump him."

"I said shad up, all of yous! I hate all of yous!" Buzzsaw climbed down the stairs as far as the full extent of his chain would allow, silencing the dogs into a reluctant hush. "And I can't wait to lock my jaws around one of your scrawny little necks so I can snap it."

Brisk cautioned Needlenose under his breath. "Go easy now."

"This guy hates everything," one of the dogs whispered. "He's a mean one. Remember what he did to Striker, Maxwell, and Skip?"

Someone shouted, "Yeah, the big bum. I'll never forget. Snapped poor Maxwell in two!"

"The lug is twisted with a couple screws loose, Needlenose," Worm acknowledged. "He's plain evil personified. He hates everything—humans, dogs, birds, cats, cars, trash cans."

Buzzsaw began growling long and hard as silence descended on the basement. With a feeling of dominance, he slowly walked back up the stairs.

The dogs breathed sighs of relief as Whiskey, a bulldog, spoke up, "I don't see why Tony keeps that mutt anyway. All he is, is a killer!"

"Tony keeps him to keep us in line," someone shouted.

"I seen Buzzsaw once nearly tear this burglar in two," another dog said. "I kid you not, boys. He nearly ripped 'im in two! The dog is dangerous! How can Tony keep such an animal?"

Needlenose answered, "Because he's an animal himself, is why. Keeps us down here to fight and make him rich. He don't care nothing 'bout us, whether we live or die in that ring!"

"Hey now, that's not altogether true," Brisk stepped in. "He feeds us good, cares for us somewhat, and we're able to stretch our legs outside once in a while—"

"Oh yeah?" Needlenose asked. "So what? While we're slowly tearing each other apart down here, none of us lives a long life, always aching and bruised."

"Look, it's a part of show biz, ain't it?" Brisk looked at Needlenose. "Listen, you and me could be out on the streets, cold and starving with no place to go. Or we could be owned by Cadillac Bill, and you know how he treats his dogs!"

"Yeah, gouges them with sticks and starves them to fight!" someone yelled.

"That's right, so you see, we all are lucky in a sense. Look, all we have to do is what we been doing. No cheap shots, no nasty biting, but always give them a good show no matter what, with lots of vicious snarls and growls. Take it easy and we should all live bearable lives."

"Hear that, you youngsters over there?" Worm shouted. "Take it easy."

"Sure, and when this place finally gets busted—believe me, it will—we'll be placed into a pet adoption service, we'll all have good homes with loving people, and we can finally retire."

Brisk looked hopeful and dreamlike, visualizing what he'd said as he scanned the numerous tired, aged, encaged gladiators. "What you old timers always dreamed about: no more fighting, just days in large, spacious backyards for scratching and digging, fetching balls with your youthful masters, chewing large bones in the summer sunlight, being petted for just being—well, being you—and having a bowl with your name on it."

"Ugh!" Needlenose grunted disbelievingly as he nuzzled inside his bowl. "Don't start us on that pipe dream again. 'Sides, what makes you think Tony and these sloshed lugs that come to bet on us are any different than the rest of them humans? I hate 'em all."

"Needlenose, I'm surprised at ya," one of the dogs said. "Soon you're gonna start hating us too, then you'll be another Buzzsaw!" The dogs howled their disapproval.

"I believe there are some kind humans out there," Brisk explained, "who are even kinder than Tidbit, who'd put up with old salty dogs like Worm and me. Homes, especially for the youngsters, with energetic kids just waiting to play. You see, guys, we can't think of ourselves as individuals in our situation. We all have to pull together—now more than ever—to give 'em a good show. What's a cut here, a little blood there, or a bruise here, from time to time? If we see it through, working together, then when we get pulled from this joint, we go to our separate homes. We'll have our freedom, find love, and be taken good care of."

"Still sounds like a pipe dream ta me!" Needlenose stubbornly disagreed, with his mouth still in his tray.

Suddenly, without warning, Buzzsaw rushed downstairs after them, but luckily his chain tensed to its breaking point part way down the stairs and snapped him back.

Startled, the dogs were horror-stricken and became silent.

Buzzsaw's growl turned into a harsh ominous wail as he disappeared back beyond the stairs.

Worm whispered to Brisk, "I think our boy's in a bad way."

"Yeah, I know."

"You don't get the gist of what I'm telling you, ole boy. I think it's quite clear that Buzzsaw up there has got the 'sickness.'"

"Yeah he's sick!"

"No, lad, he has the 'sickness.' Look into his eyes ... that crazy gaze."

"What? Worm, are you ... ?"

"Shhhh, trust me. I've seen it twice in the seven kennels I've had to display my fighting skills in, and, by Joe, he's got it."

Both dogs, suddenly shivering, curled up on the bottom of their kennels and looked toward the landing in the cold darkness where Buzzsaw had stood, before lapsing into sleep.

The next day, the handlers took the dogs out in teams for one of their rare daytime walks around the yard. This was a reward all in itself. The dogs relished the sunlight that some were once familiar with, the trees, the grass, and the feeling of the wind blowing through their fur and tickling their noses. Muzzled, Brisk and Worm were led out to walk together. Brisk, hearing Tidbit's voice, was delighted to see the boy stopping by for a visit on his return from school.

One of the handlers spoke, "Hey ya, Tidbit, what's shaking? How was school? Still cranking out those A's to be a lawyer?" Handing Brisk's and Worm's leashes over to him, he continued, "I know you wanna walk your dog."

Tidbit's buddies and other school children loved to stand by and marvel as he walked the dogs. Brisk walked the length of the yard stepping taller, with his chest sticking out.

The handler then walked downstairs for another team.

Inside the bar, Tony was in an ever-resurfacing conversation with one of his employees.

"I'm telling you, boss, we need more dogs in here—more aggressive and savage, like Cadillac Bill's and Silk Stocking's. Now, they draw a crowd!"

"Mickey, I think my dogs are good enough," Tony spoke, wearing his signature hat and smoking a cigar.

"No, they're not, boss, they're not even bloody enough. A lot of the bettors are complaining. A lot of 'em want to see more blood and carnage, to see our dogs fight to the death like Cadillac Bill's and those over on Harper Street."

"No, now I definitely refuse that. There is no way I'll have any dogs under my care fighting to the death. That's too cruel. Besides, I believe even dogs have feelings. They have a right to live."

"Yes, boss, that's nice, but look at the big-time wagers Cadillac Bill's dogs are getting. They're in the big-time making big bucks, while we stand to lose—"

"Okay, Mickey," Tony finally conceded to pacify Mickey and end the discussion. "We'll get more dogs, but I'll have none of those killing wagers in my business!"

Mickey, feeling he won a small victory in his attempt to win the boss over, knew that eventually he'd wear Tony down. Besides, this was a business, a very lucrative after-hours business. Top fighting dogs brought their owners and breeders good money. The paying public always had a hunger for the unusual: sideshow acts, brutal sports, even killing. Dogfighting brought it all, including the impending life-or-death matches that many of the humans fantasized about, giving them a rush much like the rush possibly felt by the spectators of the Roman gladiator battles thousands of years ago. And for the promoter housing such big-draw events, admission alone could be tens of thousands of dollars profit, not to mention the wagering on the dogs, the additional card and dice gambling, liquor, and other red-light activities. But the dogfights were the main purse. They were the main draw that made everything else fall neatly into place. Mickey, feeling victorious, looked over to a growling Buzzsaw.

Glancing at Buzzsaw, Tony said, "Hey ya, whatzzamatter, Buzzsaw, baby? Why you so down? Mickey, give 'im some water. He's slobbering."

Mickey cautiously held the water dish in front of Buzzsaw. The dog looked at the water, turned away, then viciously leaped at Mickey, knocking the bowl to the ground.

"Crazy mutt, I oughta brain you with this bottle!" Mickey shouted, grabbing a pint of liquor from behind the bar.

"Leave 'im alone, Mickey. Dogs have their days too, you know."

Buzzsaw continued to bare his fangs as the hair on his back stood on end.

* * *

Days passed and it was now Friday night. Brisk stood in his cage, ready for his upcoming match. "After tomorrow night, we'll have a four-day weekend, Worm, old buddy."

Worm, with a nagging itch, continuously scratched himself with his rear paw. "Yeah, Brisk, but you see the new talent the boss is fresh on recruiting?"

"Yeah, so what?"

"Have you noticed the pups are a bit on the vicious side?"

"Yeah, well, we'll have to have a chat with the new ones. Tell them the way things work here at Tony's."

The handler took Brisk out of his cage for the face-off, and Brisk gave a snarl of anticipation.

A new pit bull, which had been placed inside the small, confined ring, snarled and bit at Brisk. The dog's handler hung on for the bell as the spectators placed their wagers.

From a prone position, Brisk looked into the newcomer's eyes. "Hey there, buddy. You've got some nasty cuts on you. The name's Brisk. Don't worry; I'll go easy on you. Let's give 'em a show now!"

The dog looked at him and growled, "Shut up, you! Yous better worry about the bruises you're gonna receive, 'cause I'm gonna rip you to shreds!"

Brisk was surprised to hear the dog speak with such anger.

Without warning, the dog jumped out of its handler's hands and attacked Brisk, who was still being held. The spectators cheered as Brisk attempted to fight the other dog off—at a disadvantage, still tightly leashed.

The dog chomped down on Brisk's neck. Brisk yelped. Brisk's handler, out of self-defense, let him loose.

Brisk snarled at his attacker, "You idiot! Are you crazy? What are you trying to do?"

Brisk attempted diplomacy and tried with difficulty to safely pin the dog down as to not further injure the already badly mistreated animal. He was shocked to feel the dog release its grip, only to viciously clamp onto his eyebrow, tearing it open.

"Ouch!" Brisk yelped in pain, finding it hard to believe the damage the new dog had done. Out of anger and fear of losing limbs, Brisk quickly force clamped the dog's throat like a locking vise, suffocating it more with each ounce of pressure he applied. The dog begged surrender. The handlers broke up the fight as the spectators gave the match rousing approval with a standing ovation.

While one of the handlers tried treating his open wound, Brisk, standing atop the kennel, asked, "What's wrong with that new dog? Is he crazy? He tried to rip my darn eye out!"

"I tried cautioning you, ole boy," Worm told him. "We're going to have to have a discussion with the new ones as soon as possible, but until then, if you'd pardon my pun, we'll have to keep an eye out for them."

Brisk didn't find this comment the least bit funny as he grimaced while the handler placed pressure on his bleeding wound.

* * *

As the night's last bout concluded and the last spectator left, Mickey rejoiced in the earnings. "Look, boss, tonight we made a killing."

"Yes, we did do good, but we got three dogs badly injured and one possibly crippled! If this keeps up, I won't have any dogs to fight. Besides, I can't afford to keep paying for stitches like Brisk and Whitehair will need."

"Why pay for stitches, boss, when next week, they'll only open them up again? Besides, if you get more vicious dogs, you'll get more money. You get more money, you push the fights back to just once a week. This will, in turn, get a bigger build up. More people'll come out, which means even more money!"

"But the dogs will be more mangled. Did ya figger that in your 'more money' mathematics, Mickey? They wouldn't survive even two weeks!"

"You hear that?" A concerned and still bleeding Whitehair coughed. "They're gonna kill us—kill us all!"

"No, they're not going to kill you—I will!" one of the new dogs shouted, to everyone's surprise.

The dogs began to bark in discontent. "Now you see here, now that's the wrong attitude, mate! We gotta work together, not against each other," another dog answered.

"I only know how to survive in this fight world, and that's what I'm gonna do until I drop over with the likes of one of you standing over my dead body!" the new dog answered.

Brisk beseechingly said, "Come on, you new guys, this is precisely the thing we're trying to prevent."

"Listen, boss," Mickey said, still trying to reason. "You're getting soft. You're becoming too fond of those dogs. You gotta remember this is a business!"

The dogs barked their disapproval at the new recruits as Whitehair, disoriented from pain and having enough of the fighting and arguing, noticed that the care handler forgot to lock his kennel after treating him. Whitehair went unnoticed amidst the heated argument until he opened his cage.

"What are you doing?" Whiskey yelled.

"I'm clearing out of here. I'm escaping!"

"You can't do that, Whitehair! You won't make it past Buzzsaw. He'll kill you," Brisk cautioned.

Whitehair wasn't hearing that. He was injured and only wanted out. Bolting up the stairs with the dogs barking at him to halt, he disappeared out of sight.

"No, Whitehair, don't do this! Come back, I beg of you!" his friend Whiskey pleaded.

The dogs heard a tortured yelp, then silence. All watched as Buzzsaw's silhouette walked to the top of the stairs, dangling Whitehair's body from his mouth. The dogs froze.

Buzzsaw chomped his massive jaws into Whitehair's back, breaking him, then dropped Whitehair to the floor. And if this wasn't enough, Buzzsaw then kicked his dead body down the stairs, where Whitehair's body lay crumpled and broken. The dogs raised such a ruckus in protest that it caught the attention of Tony and Mickey.

Whiskey, harshly impacted by the horror, had been a kennel mate and friend to Whitehair for as long as he could remember. The act Buzzsaw committed was simply intolerable.

"Not even a dog should die like that," Whiskey said. With the courage afforded to his lineage of bulldogs, Whiskey charged his kennel gate, ramming it with his head once, twice, three times, until the cage fell onto the floor and he was free. He slowly walked over to his best friend's crumpled body, and with a low menacing snarl, he stepped over it and stood at the foot of the basement stairs, scouring the darkness for Buzzsaw. Whiskey was oblivious to the refraining shouts of his friends around him. Charging up the stairs, he viciously attacked Buzzsaw, catching him off guard.

The caged spectators' moods swayed toward cheering as Whiskey continued besting the huge bully. "Give it to him good, Whiskey!"

"Give 'im one for Whitehair and Maxwell!" another shouted.

Whiskey, strong, sturdy, and low to the ground, confused Buzzsaw with his fighting technique. Lashing out, Whiskey's crushing jaws latched onto Buzzsaw's rear left leg, which caused Buzzsaw to yelp. The caged animals screamed with elation hearing Buzzsaw's whimper.

Whiskey put up a good fight, but he was still winded, having fought a bout earlier. Buzzsaw, correcting his fault, was now getting the better of him, ripping savagely at the top of his head and his neck, but Whiskey's stubborn, tough hide stood up to Buzzsaw. He continued brawling when others would have run for their lives.

Buzzsaw was on top of Whiskey, dominating him, but Whiskey still refused to yield. Brisk and the rest of his friends voiced their outrage once again.

Tony and Mickey finally interceded and, with great effort, had to pry Buzzsaw's locked jaws from the top of Whiskey's badly mauled head. Whiskey, rising up on all fours, slowly walked with dignity down the stairs without making a sound. An eerie silence filled the basement. Standing over his fallen buddy with long sorrowful eyes, his breathing deepened. Whiskey was bleeding badly. He looked back up at Buzzsaw, who had been carrying on wildly upstairs.

Whiskey lay down, resting his head alongside Whitehair's outstretched neck. Giving a deep cleansing sigh, he said, "Don't you worry none, old buddy. Your old pal Whiskey got him one good time for you."

Whiskey slowly closed his eyes and died in that very spot. The dogs watched silently in honor at their fallen comrades.

Tony, looking over the sight, shook his head. "Look at this mess! Will you look at this mess? What has gotten into him? Is Buzzsaw crazy?"

Mickey shrugged his shoulders in confusion.

Tony, feeling regret, spoke quietly, "Get someone down there to clean it up."

Moments of lamented silence passed.

"That tears it!" Needlenose exclaimed as he battered the cage. "Buzzsaw's history. Anybody else wanting a piece of 'im can join me!" Needlenose, half bulldog himself, was determined to get his shot at the killer.

Other dogs began to join in and rattled their cages to escape. One dog raised his voice among the chaos. "Wait!" It was Worm, demanding to be heard, speaking with his characteristic elegant flair. "The situation is a bit more complex than it seems, gentlemen. Besides dealing with circumstances beyond our control, this isn't the time or the place for this."

"Listen, listen!" Brisk beseeched.

Worm continued. "To massively attack Buzzsaw now would create a great deal more pain, death, and suffering, which I say, would be more human than canine."

"What do you know?" someone shouted.

"I know that Buzzsaw just might not be the hell-bent killing brute we are overwhelmingly driven to believe—there may be other forces compelling him to such foul acts."

"Don't listen to the pompous old fool—his head is full of rocks," Needlenose exclaimed.

"Buzzsaw has the sickness!" Brisk screamed.

This admission finally got the dogs' full attention, and they ceased their ruckus and appeared docile.

"The sickness?"

"He has the sickness?"

"How could it be—?"

"It is true. He is infected with rabies, and if one of you—or all of you—attacks him right now, with one nip you'll be rabid too. So, I say to you all once again, now isn't the time. I do side with the majority and agree he must be stopped. Someone within this compound *must* do it, of course, but we all know the risk now."

A hush fell upon the kennels. Soon, the handler carried Whiskey and Whitehair away.

The next morning, one of the handlers who was checking the condition of the injured animals in the kennels for that night's bout took a careful look at Brisk's wounds. Tony and Mickey sat upstairs at the bar, preparing the wager cards for the night's fight while Buzzsaw barked relentlessly and tugged feverishly at his chain trying to get downstairs to the kennels.

Tony, annoyed by such overbearing activity, sent Mickey to check Buzzsaw. "Clobber him silly if ya have to!"

Mickey walked over with a broken broomstick as the dog still barked with his back turned to the room. Crashing the stick hard across Buzzsaw's back with his first lick, and then returning it for another swing, Mickey scolded, "Didn't cha hear, you stupid mutt? The boss says shut your trap! Shut yo—"

Buzzsaw suddenly swung around, and to Mickey's surprise, the dog didn't in the least bit resemble himself. He had been transformed. It appeared as though some unknown dark beast was chained there. White foam oozed from his mouth, covering his entire face and dripping heavily onto the floor. His eyes looked wild, and it sent a shudder of fear coursing through Mickey's body as he stepped backwards.

"Boss, boss, something's wrong here!"

Buzzsaw, as if possessed, snapped the heavy steel-reinforced chain. Baring his seemingly larger-than-life devil fangs, he leaped on Mickey. "Help me! Help me boss!"

Tony could not see the two as they fell behind the bar. "What in blazes is going on here?" Tony yelled, running towards them.

"Gun! Get your gun! Ahhh!" Mickey emitted a high pitch scream, then a gurgling sound, and then his voice was cut off.

"Oh dear, I'd say Buzzsaw's condition has worsened," Worm commented to Brisk as the handler, startled by the commotion, ceased treating him.

"What in the Sam Hill?" The handler, leaving Brisk's cell door ajar, walked toward the stairs.

Tony stared in horror as Buzzsaw's mouth loosened from Mickey's neck, the man's body motionless. The dog then slowly and menacingly turned to face him.

"Good Lord!" Tony shouted. Panicking, he ran for the gun he kept under the bar, but just as he grasped it in the palm of his hand, Buzzsaw leapt up, grabbed Tony's entire arm with his huge 160-pound frame, and shook the gun loose. The snapping of Tony's bones was so loud and so excruciating that Tony was overcome with pain and blacked out.

The handler, ascending the stairs and stepping through the doorway, saw nothing. "Boss, where are you?"

Buzzsaw, alerted, leapt on top of the bar in front of the handler and growled as the foam frothed nonstop from his clenched teeth and dripped onto the bar. Leaping at the speechless man, Buzzsaw knocked him back down the long flight of basement stairs. The handler was out cold before he reached the bottom step.

Like the quiet before the storm, a hush of nervous anticipation fell upon the dogs still locked in their kennels. Then the huge, snarling shadow lumbered over to the stairs and began its slow, deadly descent.

"The time is upon us, dear friend," Worm said. "One of us must confront Buzzsaw for the life of us all. Under these exigent circumstances, we haven't much choice. I shall volunteer my services!"

"No, Worm," Brisk answered, "my cage is open. It's in my breeding to fight a fight such as this."

"No, my lad. I have already accepted my call of duty. Open my cage."

"I can wait and sneak up on him," Brisk argued. "I'm quicker."

"But you are small. I've had the experience of defeating him once before. Now, quickly before he's on us!" Worm insisted.

Buzzsaw, standing at the bottom of the stairs, looked around at the terror-stricken faces of those that were trapped and at his mercy in the cages. Fiercely attacking the cage closest to him,

Buzzsaw besieged one of the new dogs, who screamed in vain for mercy.

"Quickly!" Worm pleaded.

Brisk was out of his cage working quietly, yet fervently, on the lock.

Buzzsaw pried back the grating and began fighting the helpless dog cornered in his cage. Worm's door, finally swinging open, knocked Brisk to the ground.

"Buzzsaw, you cowardly flea-bitten tramp, face me, someone your own size, so I can whip you like before!" Worm spoke defiantly.

The dog in the cage lay unconscious as Buzzsaw turned to face Worm.

Brisk, now by Worm's side, said, "I'm gonna help you!"

"Stand back, my friend, you're too small," Worm mumbled, not taking his eyes off his opponent. He then charged, knocking Buzzsaw to the ground. He attacked with ferocity, aiming for Buzzsaw's throat.

Brisk stood by eagerly, seeing that his friend had the situation presently under control. Worm pinned down the desperately fighting Buzzsaw and dragged him across the basement floor.

Worm, knowing he could not afford to let up the least bit, continued to pour it on. Buzzsaw, luckily catching only the side of Worm's head, sheared off his ear. This ploy allowed Buzzsaw to regain his footing.

Brisk immediately attacked Buzzsaw's rear right leg from behind. This caused Buzzsaw to clumsily loose his footing. Buzzsaw then reached around and snapped at Brisk—and missing—so Buzzsaw then kicked Brisk back with both hind legs.

"Stay back, Brisk!" Worm cautioned again, then charged.

The two titans combated again, this time Buzzsaw having the upper hand. Planting Worm firmly on the ground, Buzzsaw latched onto Worm's neck, violently shaking it to break it under his might. The elder Worm appeared helpless. As the captive dogs encouraged Brisk, he attacked again, this time ripping at the underside of Buzzsaw's exposed belly.

Buzzsaw released his death grip on Worm and swung around blindly, trying to attack his smaller nemesis. Brisk, like a fighting technician, speedily latched onto Buzzsaw's upper lip, bringing him reluctantly to the ground.

Worm, up and fully recovered, yelled to his buddy, "Brisk, you'd bloody well move that stubborn carcass out the way now!"

Brisk released his hold. Worm, more concerned for his smaller friend than for personal harm, grabbed Brisk and flung him loosely into a stack of empty kennels. The stack collapsed on top of Brisk as he fell.

The combatants engaged again, towering beside one another on two legs as their teeth jousted to interlock for the kill. Brisk lay helpless beneath the weight of the cages, listening as the snarls and growls continued to echo through the basement. Blocked in as he was, Brisk was unable to see, but he heard the whimpering screams of his buddy three times. Then he heard the bar door upstairs swing open.

The sound also grabbed Buzzsaw's attention, and he temporarily ceased his onslaught. Brisk listened carefully to the unmistakable voice of Tidbit who, along with the other kids, must have just been let off their school bus.

"Quick, kid, it's Buzzsaw!" Tony said, regaining consciousness and holding his arm. He begged the youth, "He's gone crazy, get the police!"

Tidbit, dropping his books, ran back out the door.

Brisk fought to pull himself out of the jumble of cages as Buzzsaw climbed the stairs and bolted after the boy. Brisk broke free, running over to view a badly mangled Worm.

Worm muttered, "Think he's knocked the fight out of me, old chum. Broke both my hind legs. Looks like you're gonna have to hop to it."

Brisk cleared the top of the stairs and saw the bar door wide open as he caught sight of the tail end of Buzzsaw in pursuit of his beloved human friend, Tidbit.

"Open my cage! Open my cage!" Needlenose urged a badly crippled Worm.

Worm feebly attempted to liberate Needlenose as the other dogs encouraged him, howling to be set free to assist Brisk.

Tidbit ran, shouting warnings and calls for help, scattering the children further ahead in his path. Looking behind him, he saw the berserk dog nearly upon him, nipping at his heels.

Being fleet of foot, Brisk viciously and intentionally latched onto Buzzsaw's left hind leg, the same leg Whiskey had injured during his losing struggle. Buzzsaw fell to the ground. Brisk did not intend in the slightest to loosen his grip and remained glued to Buzzsaw as they both, resembling a ball, rolled end over end. Buzzsaw snapped, grabbed Brisk's back quarter leg, and ground with fury, but Brisk, snarling, held on bravely. What he had spoken of earlier was true—his breed was bred for this purpose only and were revered for their tolerance of pain. Both dogs stood their ground, locked in their position for several moments.

Tidbit, with four other children, had escaped towards an alley, and Buzzsaw sought a more meaningful prize. Breaking from his hold, Buzzsaw got up and pulled Brisk across the ground as if the valiant dog provided no resistance whatsoever. Brisk dragged his hind feet and finally positioned them to enable him to back pedal, trying to stop the huge, maniacal killer in vain. Buzzsaw effortlessly hauled him into the alley.

The children were trapped. Running blindly in fear, they were fenced in by a barbed-wire fence that surrounded the huge corporate buildings on both sides.

Brisk, seeing what lay ahead, knew he would be a fool to face Buzzsaw head on. With those monstrous jaws, there was no question that Buzzsaw would chew him whole. As the deranged dog came dangerously close to the screaming children,

Brisk released his grip, jumping onto Buzzsaw's back. He latched hold to Buzzsaw's upper lip but, this time, Brisk also managed to clamp onto Buzzsaw's sensitive, soft, fleshy nose, which induced unbearable wrenching pain.

Running in circles like a merry-go-round, shaking the small, persistent dog wildly into the air, Buzzsaw abruptly stopped, sending Brisk twirling into the air as the children looked on, terrified at the violent snarling dogs that were now both foaming at the mouth.

Tidbit, cheering with confidence, yelled, "Get him, Brisk! Don't let him hurt us!"

Both combatants experienced temporary dizziness from Buzzsaw's attempt to loosen Brisk and crashed at the feet of Tidbit. Buzzsaw climbed quickly to his feet, and Brisk stood ready on the approach. Brisk boldly charged to maul Buzzsaw's front legs as the huge dog clumsily jumped backward to protect them.

Standing prone, baring teeth on a head-on, face-to-face confrontation, Brisk had little choice and leapt at the other dog's throat. Buzzsaw grabbed him in midair, catching the broad, thick, top collar of Brisk's neck, and shook him violently. Brisk resembled a rag doll being tossed every which way.

Tidbit cried in horror seeing his dog tortured so. "Let my dog go! Leave us alone!"

Buzzsaw slammed Brisk to the ground, holding on for moments at a time and shaking Brisk intermittently to drain the very life out of him. Finally, Buzzsaw let go and glowered down at Brisk's very still body lying on the ground before him. To Buzzsaw's surprise, Brisk revived and leapt again for Buzzsaw's throat, wagging his tail.

Buzzsaw latched onto Brisk's back this time, crushing and shaking the pint-sized dog even longer, which opened up a deep gash on the side of Brisk's rib cage. Tossing the dog aside again for dead, Buzzsaw turned to his trapped prey, causing the children to scream louder.

Buzzsaw, breathing hard due to his injuries and energy drained from battle, appeared to smile a smile of impending doom rather than snarl. Springing forth once again like magic, a dedicated Brisk refused to go under. He stood with his back to the surprised children, snapping and barking, separating Buzzsaw from them. Buzzsaw growled in frustration. To the amazement of the children, Brisk's tail continued to wag as he panted and eagerly yapped, encouraging the monster on.

The huge Buzzsaw approached. Brisk sprang into the air once more.

Buzzsaw viciously captured his front leg, severing it clear off. Brisk, in the same motion, powerfully snagged underneath the soft part of Buzzsaw's throat, tearing and twisting with every ounce of super canine strength his breed were known to possess. Those few moments seemed like hours to the terrified children, as miraculously Buzzsaw, finally yielding, fell down.

Brisk stubbornly refused to let go. As Buzzsaw helplessly bellowed for air, Brisk tightened his grip, twisting his jaws around even further.

Worm, under extreme duress, had somehow opened two of the cages, and Needlenose and others rushed to the scene, which had tragically already ended. A passing patrol car had driven by, and the frantic cries and waving hands of the children caught the officer's attention. Running over to the still bitterly scrapping dogs, the police, for safety, shot them both.

Tidbit was grief stricken and cried, picking up his dog. Needlenose and the other two dogs huddled in front of the youth, embracing their fallen friend. But unbeknownst to Tidbit, the injuries Brisk had incurred from his battle were more fatal than the gunshot.

Time passed, and the kids' story spread from neighborhood to neighborhood about the heroic dog that saved them, courageously forfeiting his own life in battle against a rabid dog from the illegal dogfighting ring. The neighborhood block club overwhelmingly voted to adopt all of Tony's mistreated fight dogs and bestowed honor by placing them all within good homes.

Many miles away, Needlenose now sits in a huge backyard with a doghouse and even has his name on a bowl, just like Brisk once told him he would. He still gets choked up from time to time when his master brings him a large bone to leisurely chew on.

In Brisk's memory, Tidbit adopted Worm. Worm, who had his wounds treated and received numerous shots, made a simple promise. During his remaining years, he vowed to never forget his small friend who helped bring them all love from warm families and hope for a better tomorrow. Worm and Brisk were remarkably still inseparable as friends, for Brisk's gravesite was practically side-by-side with Worm's doghouse. There, for Worm's remaining few years, he lived in peace, and upon many occasions talked to his friend.

* * *

"Lord, this Brisk was surely one of your bravest fighters. How it saddens me that he was delivered to your services in part with the aid of the police."

"Well, Angel Brian, as you will witness, the police have bravely answered my faithful call countless times."

Helena

Helena, fresh out of canine police academy, was the academy's first female graduate ever. Being of bona fide German shepherd ancestry, she was listed categorically by Canine Fanciers as a "police dog." She was honored to carry on a long family tradition, which extended to a brother working for St. Clair Shores police and two other brothers working for county police in the southern states. Make no bones about it; she proudly carried the torch of being the city's first female police dog and her family's first female to ever serve as such.

Helena, at two years old, was considered a striking beauty. With a solidly thick build, she displayed a typical dark black coat with white fur underneath, marked like all true police dogs. Yet, distinguishing her from other police dogs were her glamorous white markings about the face and a cute noticeable mole, which added a pleasing feminine touch.

Helena still remembered the first day she was led to the canine unit building where she would share the compound with seven of her peers. While she was escorted toward the kennels, passing through the huge building—which had polished marble floors—she looked up to the walls, glancing at ancient pictures of award-winning police dogs with their masters receiving citations, plaques, and ribbons for outstanding work in the call of duty. She did not consider herself truly alone, for of the seven dogs at the compound, two had also recently graduated with her. One of the dogs in particular, she took a fancy to. His name was Champ.

Champ, a picturesque and handsome brown and black German sheperd, exuded the essence of strength. Helena, judging by his looks and how he moved with such grace and fluidity, thought he was well named. She remembered him walking by her in the academy and how she would gasp and her heart would flutter, secretly choosing in her mind, without a doubt, that he would be the perfect mate for her.

For Champ, it was hard to go unnoticed by either human-kind or dogs. With his sturdy muscular body and bold stance, he looked like he was molded out of tungsten steel. People quite naturally admired and reached out to pet such a fine animal.

Helena, feeling terribly shy at the academy, never truly had the chance to speak to him. Sure, he cast a glance now and then or, like the other dogs from the suburban classes, made a comment or two at her being the only female, but he never spoke directly to her.

It seemed it was going to all work out fine until she met the other dogs in the kennel. One day, they gave her a really rough time for being female.

Boris, one of the oldest German shepherds in the kennel, croaked, "What're you doing here, ya skirt? This here's a man's job. You should be somewhere guarding someone's house!"

"Or at home somewhere having pups. You look too stupid to be guarding someone's business," Satch, another shepherd, spoke.

This brought laughter to the older dogs.

"Heck, all this broad's gonna do is get in the way and louse up things," Shemp, another shepherd, added. "Trust me, a female's nothing but bad luck!" He chuckled as he slapped his paw upon the shoulder of Torchy, another academy classmate of Helena's.

Torchy hesitated as Shemp asked, "Ain't that right, pal?"

"Well, I don't know if I could say that. I mean, I don't know if it's been proven yet," Torchy answered.

At that, all the dogs laughed. Torchy's comment even brought a mild chuckle from Champ.

"I don't know whether or not she's bad luck, but I oughta make her fetch into the kitchen and cook me a batch of doggy biscuits," Satch said threateningly, which made every one laugh even more.

Boris gloated, seeing Champ join in the laughter, while Tor-chy, glancing at Helena, could see her discomfort and ceased laughing.

Boris noticing the rather tickled yet poised shepherd, Champ, spoke, "Hey bud, you seem like an okay Joe. It's good to have another of your kind here."

"What? What is this? What is this here?" asked a dog breaking through the group that was all alongside Helena's kennel. The dog, named Pierre, was an exotic French hound distinguishingly bred in Japan. He was a tall, black, handsome looking dog, with a pretty, shiny black coat, black eyes, and a long skinny tail.

"We have the new recruits here. Splendid!" Looking at Helena as the dogs continued their insults, Pierre commented, "Well, at least it's nice to know I will no longer be the black sheep!"

The dogs howled with laughter as Helena moped away feeling miserable.

"Come on, fellas," Boris invited, "let's go over to my doghouse. I've got plenty of chow."

As the group left still laughing, Torchy ran after Helena. "Hey, Helena, it's me, Torchy." Seeing her emotional face, he could see that she was fighting to hold back tears. "Don't take it so hard. The guys were just poking fun at you. They didn't mean it."

"Yeah, sure."

Torchy, running back toward the crowd, turned and said, "I gotta go. Talk to you later."

"Sure."

Helena walked quietly around the large yard. She had no idea her first day at the canine unit kennels would be like this. Looking out beyond the fence into the city, she dreaded spending five days a week training here and suddenly missed her master, Winston, a police officer who was married to a pretty woman named Gloria. They had two adorable kids, a boy and a girl, with whom, up to this point, Helena exclusively shared a small bricklayered home.

As the day drew to a close, Helena missed them even more. That night, while the others lay in their kennels talking and joking into the wee hours of the morning, she never felt so alone lying in her doghouse. She couldn't wait to go back to her real home.

The week of training and ridicule dragged by until the weekend, when Helena was eager to go home. As her master, Winston, brought her inside their home, Gloria had a look of concern. "Honey, she doesn't look well. Look at her eyes."

"It's probably the rigorous training they put her through every day. She'll be okay. She'll get plenty of rest here."

Gloria, reaching for the doggie treats, gently petted her. "The poor dear."

The kids, Chris and Terri, ran to greet Helena and petted her generously as her tail gave a lackluster wag.

When the weekend ended, Helena, not of her choosing, returned to the unit like the other dogs. Torchy spoke briefly to her while the dogs welcomed her with continued badgering. Walking back to her doghouse, she noticed a vacant spot next to hers just on the other side of a fence, and she remembered that there had been a vacant doghouse sitting there opposite the fence. She thought nothing more of it, but at the sun's early rise, she observed that the kennel had been returned to the exact same spot.

Thinking it being nothing but strange, she switched her attention to the day's torturous training session and the abuse with which she would be pelted. Over the week, the training sessions became even more intense, leading up to the weekend, and she was again grateful to be home in a pleasant atmosphere and able to enjoy a well-deserved rest.

Upon returning to the academy the following week, she noticed again the peculiar absence of the doghouse. Then like clockwork as before, the next morning, it magically reappeared. Her curiosity piqued, Helena sniffed the rear of the doghouse as she had done with all the others from time to time, and like the rest, this house didn't give off any unusual scents.

She continued her strenuous days of training, finishing up the week in a training session outside the compound. The dogs had to leap across two high buildings, attached to a safety line in case they had the misfortune to fall. All the dogs in training jumped from the first building. Faced with a longer distance jump, the dogs approached the next obstacle. Boris, Pierre, and Shemp cleared it first, serving as role models, then Satch, Champ, and Torchy cleared it with little to no problem. Helena, who had been staring down to the far away ground since Shemp had cleared the jump, was frightened.

"Come on!" the three human trainers urged her. "Come on jump! You can do it."

Helena's shortcomings—of course—struck up a howl with the male dogs. "The chicken, lily-livered brat," Satch spoke. "I told ya she was a coward. How could ya trust something like that to be by your side?"

"She can't be trusted," Shemp commented. "All females are bad luck, like I said!"

The three trainers continued to urge her on. While fearing more for her safety than rejection, Torchy shouted encouragement. "Come on, Helena, you can do it! No sweat. It's easy!"

Helena, getting a grip, figured she hadn't much choice. If she refused, the guys would definitely label her as coward, a label that would get spread throughout the entire police community. Furthermore, the police trainers might feel that she was unacceptable for the canine unit and recommend her termination from the program, leaving her to be an embarrassing blemish on the family name. Helena was more than convinced she must jump.

Backing up a bit, she looked at the trainers' waiting arms over on the other side. Backing a bit more, she planned to run with all her might, then close her eyes and jump. The dogs began to quiet down, all except for Torchy, who continued to mumble words of encouragement.

Running in a full gallop towards the end of the building, Helena closed her eyes, leaping two steps too early. Opening her eyes in mid-air, she suddenly noticed she was going to fall short.

Panicking, as the force of gravity carried her downward, she screamed.

Champ and Torchy exhaled a shocked breath and watched helplessly as she plummeted. Finally, the line took up the slack and snapped taunt, ending her fall. She dangled, whimpering in terror.

"That stupid little skirt. I ought to snip that line myself," Boris commented.

The other dogs continued grumbling.

With two trainers pulling her up as she hovered above the third one, never had Helena felt such embarrassment and trauma. As the trainers hoisted her up, she shook with fear and tucked her tail between her legs.

Pierre, in a surprising show of sympathy said, "You guys should lighten up a bit. That was indeed quite a distant to jump."

"Yeah, and she coulda been killed too!" Torchy said, running to her side.

Boris mockingly said, "Oh, and then where would us lugs be without another skirt to help us along in this cruel world?"

The dogs walked ahead towards the stairwell with two of the trainers. Torchy was still consoling Helena when Champ doubled back on them.

"Glad you're okay, but it would help matters if you'd stop being such a pup!"

Helena was surprised, as this statement was the first true words Champ had spoken to her face. Then like his approach, he immediately left to join the merrymaking group.

Returning back to the unit, Helena was the first one out of the canine van, and she ran directly to her doghouse. She refused to eat and decided not to leave that spot until Winston picked her up the next day for the weekend.

It was dark, but Helena, unable to sleep, gazed at the stars and thought about the events of the day. It was all becoming tremendously hard for her to cope with. As she lay thinking, much to her surprise, a grunting sound—like someone clearing his throat—breached the late night silence. Shocked, she looked around, moving only her eyes left to right, feeling the stranger so close, almost as if he was right upon her. Then she heard a long, deep, dwindling sigh that faded into silence. At first Helena was uncertain, but now she was dead sure; it sounded like something was right next to her.

She got up, figuring it could be Boris or Satch attempting to pull a prank or trying to frighten her. Leaving her kennel, she carefully stepped into the night air, threatening to attack whoever was to assume she was so vulnerable for such a joke. However, upon looking around she noticed all the other dogs fast asleep and more than comfortable in their respective dreamlands. She didn't know whether this situation puzzled or frightened her.

Walking back to her doghouse, she looked at the empty, isolated doghouse fenced out alongside of hers. Cautiously inching up to it, she sniffed it carefully, then after a moment of silence, she spoke. "Hello, is anyone in there? Hello, is anyone there? Are you listening?" She received no answer. She walked into her kennel then abruptly walked out to look about curiously. "Nothing."

Giving up, she returned to her doghouse. Unsettled, she turned herself around in three circles then comfortably lay down. She was determined to keep a sharp ear out, listening even after she fell into sleep.

The next day Winston was late picking her up, but by nightfall, she was home. "Sorry honey, I'm a little late and all. You know I'm working on that Slasher case—"

"My God, I've seen it on the news. It's his sixth victim. Do you have any leads?" Gloria questioned.

Just then, breaking from the den where they had been playing video games, Chris and Terri ran into the living room to greet Daddy and Helena. Winston picked up both of his children with one swoop, laughing, then put them across either shoulder.

"Daddy missed you kids so much he might lose control hugging his precious little rug rats!" With that, Winston joyfully squeezed them, applying a tighter than normal hug as they yelled with laughter. He smothered them both with affectionate kisses.

Gloria, changing the subject since the kids were present, petted Helena. "How is our darling doing? We're beginning to miss our best four-legged friend. Oh dear, she's not looking well. Sweetheart, take a look at our Helena!" Gloria started to become emotional.

Winston placed the kids down gently, and they ran over to pet Helena. Terri, the youngest, questioned, "Mommy, is Helena gonna die?"

"Of course not, my little pumpkin."

Winston spoke, "Let me take a look."

The kids parted, giving their father room while they rubbed Helena's huge back. Winston, doing a quick check over, said, "She appears okay, doesn't look hurt or bruised."

"Look into her eyes, dear. She looks traumatized or something."

Taking a closer look, he stated, "No, maybe she's just exhausted. It looks like plain exhaustion—like my eyes. See?" Winston said jokingly.

Gloria smiled.

"She'll be okay. We'll just make sure she gets plenty of rest over the weekend."

"Can she sleep in my bed this time, Dad?" Chris eagerly asked. "She slept with Terri all last weekend."

"No, she didn't. She slept on the floor one time."

"Yes, Son, she can sleep in your bed tonight," Winston answered.

Terri stomped her feet in protest, about to cry, until her mom interrupted. "I tell you what. Right after supper, you'll all share the bed and sleep together just like camp."

The children celebrated with a cheer, but then Chris voiced an embarrassing opinion. "Momma, I think Helena might not like that idea."

"And pray tell, why not, young man?" Gloria questioned.

"Terri still has a problem of wetting the bed."

"Do not! I big girl now!" Teri spoke with a pouted lip. This brought laughter from Winston as he ushered them both to the dining room table.

Helping his wife in the kitchen, Winston murmured, "No wonder Helena slept the second night on the floor in Terri's room. She's a smarter dog than I thought."

Gloria teased him by threatening him with the forks to be placed on to the table.

In the middle of the night, Winston was awakened by a terrible dream involving the Slasher. If he remembered right, he had tracked the Slasher down, and the Slasher had cornered him in a small room without his weapon. Moving slowly out of the bed so as not to disturb his wife, he quietly tiptoed out of the room.

Passing the kids' room, he observed the familiar large head protruding alertly between the sleeping kids in the dark. "So you can't sleep either, huh girl?"

Helena gently rose between the kids, only stirring Terri, as she crept out to greet her master, who sat in a chair in the front room. "Seems we both have difficult jobs—I'm frustrated, girl." Rubbing her mane to comfort her as she affectionately nuzzled against him, he spoke again. "And scared."

The two had this tender quiet time well into the morning until Gloria, surprised upon arising alone, found them both asleep, lying side by side in the front room.

The following day, Helena accompanied Gloria and the kids on a walk in the park. Winston couldn't join them, as he had been called in early to work on the Slasher case. Helena looked at Gloria and sensed that Gloria was worried but was keeping a calm face for the kids. The kids, unaware of their mother's tension, played with Helena and enjoyed their frolic-filled romp in the park.

The next day, Helena returned to the unit. On this day of training, the dogs were scheduled to practice their take-down attacks. This exercise was simply a trainer standing with a play weapon in hand and wearing a protective arm brace pad. The dogs were supposed to viciously attack, bringing the criminal to the ground. The trainer posing as the decoy stood 6'3" and weighed in close to 260 pounds, making this feat sometimes difficult for the dogs.

Boris, Satch, and Shemp, having been exposed hundreds of times to this exercise, were used to this training and brought the decoy down quickly. Pierre, a hound dog, was exempt from this exercise. The new recruits had mastered the art of grabbing and holding but found it difficult to bring the huge man down, much to the razzing of the old timers. It took Champ and Torchy a long time to get the decoy down, and for Helena, it took what seemed like hours.

"Come on ya stupid skirt! We ain't got all day. It's nearly time for supper!" Boris, yelling over the guys' laughter, added, "Speaking of supper, why don't you just give up, broad, put on the apron, and fix me some?"

Helena and the decoy were both tired when she finally flipped him to the ground. Helena's anger level peaked; she had had enough of being ridiculed. Walking up to Boris, she stood face-to-face with him, snarling. Satch and Shemp were quick to join Boris's side.

"What's the problem, ya skank? I ordered you in there to fix my supper and you ain't moving!"

Helena crouched to jump at him, but Torchy stepped in front of her just in time to block what he thought was her "foolish reaction."

"Don't you do it. Can't you see they're provoking you? Just bear with it. It'll die down soon," he whispered into her steaming ears.

"It won't. I've been here for more than a month, and all I get is the same treatment from these old windbags."

The three laughed, and Satch said, "Well, if you feel that way about it, why don't you just quit, you stupid female. We don't want you here in our group anyway!"

"Yeah," Shemp agreed. "Besides, you're bad luck!"

"You're all hard on me because you're prejudiced, and you're afraid. Afraid that I'm better than any of you, and I am!"

"Prejudiced?" Boris howled.

"Afraid?" Satch laughed.

Boris, walking up to her, said, "I'm not prejudiced. You gotta be silly. Why, there isn't a female out there that I had that I didn't like."

The dogs chuckled as Shemp added, "Yeah, we know what you mean."

"Prejudiced? Besides, if we were prejudiced, we wouldn't let old Pierre there, a Japanese Frenchman, join our group. Right men?"

Satch and Shemp both gave their affirmations. Satch concluded, "We just don't want no broads lousing up things."

Helena walked closer to Boris. "What's wrong, Boris? You afraid of me? Remember, your mother was a female, right? Or in your household, did she wear the pants too?" Torchy snickered as Boris became furious.

Immediately, Helena and Boris locked in battle. As they fought viciously about the field, the older dogs cheered Boris on. The fighting gained Pierre's attention, and he ran within the group already surrounding the combatants.

After a while, Boris got her on the ground, and Satch tried to sneak in a bite on an unsuspecting Helena. Torchy jumped to her defense, baring his fangs, daring Satch to try again. "We're keeping it a fair fight!"

Helena was losing, but she boldly fought onward.

"Hey, Boris, she's had enough," Pierre commented.

"Mind your business, you French Japanese," Shemp snapped.

They finally drew the full attention of the trainers, who had thought it was only a brief skirmish that would have ended by then.

"Boris! Boris, you cut it out, if you know what's good for you, you trouble maker!" Sherman, one of the trainers ran over to pull Boris from atop Helena. The trainer hit Boris several times, making him yelp, but Boris escaped to the other side of the yard. Helping Helena up, the trainer asked, "You okay, Helena? God, look what he's done to you! Winston is gonna have my butt. Charlie, call the vet. Poor Helena's got to get stitches. Look at this mess."

The two trainers picked the agitated Helena up, placed her inside a nearby truck, and drove to the veterinarian. "That obnoxious buffoon, look what he done to her. You don't think he permanently damaged her where she can't successfully complete the canine training, do you?"

"I don't know. I just don't know," Charlie replied.

The vet gave Helena a sedative while stitching her up. Helena slept through the whole ordeal and woke peaceably in her doghouse in the middle of the night. Stirring around for a moment, she moaned from the pain of her wounds, which jogged her memory and made her remember the previous day's event.

The weather was just right for an early June night. Not too warm or humid where the moisture stuck to Helena's fur, leaving her groping around miserable in the night, but cool enough to just stretch out and sleep. The night was clear and peaceful. Helena had nearly forgotten about the whole day and felt kind of mellow. She reasoned it must be the lingering effects of the drugs. Relaxed, she stared up into the night sky, laid her head back, and sighed deeply. She enjoyed the moment of silence.

"Muoon ... bwutiful ... toonight."

Hearing the strange voice totally surprised Helena and knocked her off guard. She didn't know who it was or what to say, yet she didn't want to feel stupid or offend the speaker by saying something wrong. Peering closely into the night sky, she gathered her courage and hesitantly spoke. "I ... I wouldn't know. I ... I mean, I can't see it from where I'm sitting."

Suddenly, she jumped, startled to feel her doghouse slowly move in small increments as a huge paw reached through the fence and turned her doghouse diagonally. She looked up, gazing at the big, bold, full moon that looked so near and so bright that she felt as though she could reach out and touch its glowing silver surface. She was mesmerized, as this was the first time she actually sat and admired the moon's alluring beauty.

"Yes, I must agree it's quite beautiful."

After a long moment of silence, the voice deeply sighed. Then it spoke in short, slowly controlled, breathy sounds, as if the voice was careful not to stumble, like maybe it was the first time it was communicating. "Y—y—you ... hound ... s—s—shepherd?"

Helena confused at first then realized that the statement was a question. "I ... I'm a German shepherd, full-blooded breed ... but my name is Helena."

The voice sighed again, and then took a long pause. Helena didn't know whether the one behind the voice heard her, had fallen asleep, or was suddenly angry and content to just ignore her again. As she sat, a thousand and one questions surfaced in her head, but she restrained herself, simply calling out one question. "You, in the kennel, please tell me your name. What's your name?"

After long moments of silence, the voice slowly spoke. "DE—AKE ... now ... sleep."

Helena waited for an hour, but she didn't hear another sound. Speaking into the night, she silently repeated to herself, "Deake?"

Helena woke late in the morning; the trainers had decided to let her rest for the day. The other dogs had already started their morning exercise. She looked around, hearing the trainers shouting commands at the dogs, and rationally thought last night's truly bizarre occurrence was a dream probably caused by the drugs that had been administered to her.

Helena got up slowly and walked out of her doghouse. She sniffed the rear of the other kennel then asked, "Deake? Deake, you there?"

No answer. She was satisfied that she had been hallucinating until she saw that the ground was moved beneath her doghouse, evidence that it had indeed been shifted. At this realization, she mumbled, "It's true and I wasn't imagining it! Deake, Deake, where are you?"

After moments of curiously waiting, she left. The dogs were scheduled a break. She walked around the yard, gaining attention, as Torchy eagerly called out to her, "Helena, Helena!" Running over, he spoke in surprise, "You're up and you're around walking. I'm glad you're okay," he added, displaying his enthusiasm to her with a welcoming, affectionate lick.

She smiled. "Of course I'm okay, Torchy."

From behind, a voice spoke, "It is good that you are, my young pup. You've caused me considerable worry."

She turned around, and to her surprise, it was a smiling Pierre who had greeted her. "Thanks Pierre, it's good to know that you care."

"Well, of course," Pierre said as he gallantly trotted back toward his training area. Helena looked at Torchy and started walking. "Come on. Let's head to the training area."

"Come on, tell me you're kidding, right?"

"Course not. Let's go."

Torchy laughed, accompanying her. Along the way, she asked, "Torchy, could you do me a big favor?"

"Anything for a pal, Helena, just name it."

"Later on, while I'm not around, of course—and don't tell them I asked—ask the other dogs about someone named Deake."

"Deake?"

"Yes, Deake, I'd appreciate it."

"Sure, ah, don't mention it."

Sherman was astonished to see her and walked over to gently pet her. "Hey, girl, what you doing up and on your feet already? The vet said you should get at least two days' rest."

Another trainer, Charlie, spoke, "Hey, Sherman, you didn't think a few nasty cuts would hold Helena down. Heck, she's a real trooper!"

Charlie joined in greeting Helena as Sherman replied, "Yeah, Charlie, you might be right. Here I thought she wouldn't make it. She's got spunk. Hey, girl, know of any human female counterparts like you? I'm looking to be hitched."

The trainers laughed then assembled all the dogs for their course of workouts. Champ briefly smiled admiringly at the rejuvenated Helena. At the day's end, the dogs reassembled into their cliques. Boris's group was, of course, caught up in the usual signifying. Torchy casually wondered over after toying with a soccer ball. As the dogs chuckled at a joke, Torchy broke in, asking a question, "Say guys, who's Deake?"

"Deake?" Boris questioned, then the name jogged his memory. "Deake ... oh, Deake you're talking about. Ha, ha, he's an idiot."

"Deake?" Shemp put on a false face, pretending to recall. "Oh yeah, that Deake, to the best of my recollection, he's a klutz."

They all began laughing aloud.

Boris spoke to Torchy. "Don't you mind that old fool, he's touched."

The group howled with laughter as they changed the subject. As the evening drew near, Helena sat inside her doghouse and ate from her bowl while Torchy approached. "I came over to see how you're doing."

"Just fine, Torchy. You care to share from my bowl?"

He smiled. "No, I've got plenty at my kennel, thanks. I've just come over to greet you before I turn in early. It should be another long day tomorrow. Oh, I got that information you asked about."

Helena, eager to hear it, jumped up quickly. "Let's walk out here." After fifty steps or so, she asked, "What did you find?"

"Well, only thing they told me was that Deake is an old fool and I should ignore him because he's crazy."

"Is that it?"

"That's about the size of it, from President Boris and his gang of misfits. Surely you weren't expecting much more."

Helena, thinking, replied, "Well, no, not really."

"Well, I'm turning in. You'd better rest up for tomorrow too. See ya."

"Yeah, thanks, Torchy. I'll see you in the morning." Helena returned to her home after she finished eating and fell fast asleep. Waking up in the late-night hours, she called out, "Deake . . . Deake? You awake, Deake? Are you around?" After a while, she heard a slow stir then a sigh. Patiently, she awaited an answer. And then he spoke.

"Deake . . . slee . . . ep."

Helena didn't disturb him further that night. The next day, the dogs left for a remote training facility. Upon their return late in the day, they found Pierre relaxing, as he had already completed his search and smell operation conducted at the unit. Helena courteously approached him. Pierre greeted her with, "Hey ya, Helena, you're still holding up?"

"Yes, I'm okay. Say, Pierre, could you tell me about some-one?"

Pierre looked at her quizzically. "Sure, what someone you want to know about?"

"Could you tell me about Deake?"

Pierre, looking surprised that she had mentioned Deake's name, felt somewhat uncomfortable. "Deake, huh? I'll have to tell you another day about Deake."

Looking disappointed, he walked off.

Helena, overwhelmed with curiosity about the shroud of mystery surrounding Deake, decided to not give up just yet. Late that night, Helena called out to him. "Deake? Deake, you feel like talking?" She waited in silence for half an hour, about to give up, when she heard, "Night ... sss beaut ... full ... qqqquiet."

Helena smiled to hear her late-night friend's voice. They talked slowly—practically all night—about the hidden beauty of the night. The stars, moon, and the way the clouds played in the sky. The different sounds in the night air: crickets chirping, dogs howling, people singing in the night. Helena, feeling more comfortable, asked a more personal question. "Deake, why is your voice—why do you talk funny?"

"F ... fffought ... wiredd ... mmm ... mouth."

She paused, then asked another question. "Everyone's master picks them up at the end of the week; why is it I never see your master, Deake?"

Deake, slow to answer, tried to form words. "Ffffssrrrrnaster ... sss ... sh ... shot ... d ... dead."

Helena felt sorrow, feeling his tragedy. If her master Winston was ever taken away, she wouldn't know what to do.

"D ... D ... De ... Deake ... sleep."

Helena, not wanting to push him, granted his rest. For the next two days it was back to training again. Deake didn't answer Helena's beckoning call for those two nights, and she began to worry.

As night fell, having thought up all the possible reasons as to why she was being ignored, Helena felt it was important to explain to him that she only wanted to help him. Helen attempted again.

"Deake, Deake, you don't have to talk if you're mad at me for asking you those questions. I understand. Really, I do, and I'm sorry if I hurt you. Just say something so that I know you're all right." She waited. There was still no answer. "I'm leaving tomorrow for the weekend. If you don't answer, I'll worry all weekend about you!"

"S ... sss ... se ... seen ... you ... tt ... today."

Helena was shocked. "You did?"

"S ... s ... se ... seen ... you ... ev ... ever ... everyda ... daday."

"Really! How?"

"Yy ... y ... you're ... b ... b ... be ... beauti ... ful."

Flattered, she smiled. "Oh, that was so kind, thank you. You must be beautiful too!"

"Nn ... n ... no ... Deake ... ug ... ug ... ugly!"

"Oh, how could you say such a thing when you see such beauty in the night? I'll bet you're beautiful. You have a beautiful personality."

Helena could have sworn she heard Deake muffle a chuckle. She now felt even more compelled to further engage him in conversation. "Deake, if I ever ask you a question that offends you, I don't mean to offend you, and I apologize. But we sometimes do that when we communicate, even friends, and I wouldn't intentionally mean to hurt you, because I would like to consider you as my friend."

Deake, moved by Helena's speech, tapped the back of her doghouse with his paw. "Ffssffb ... friend."

Helena blushed, which she would pass off as a smile. Diverting the flow of the conversation to contain herself, she decided to ask him a question. "Deake, I'm going home to my master, Winston, and the other dogs are going home as well. Where do you go over the weekend?"

"K ... kkmm ... kcomman ... der ... kkkeepss ... cckcompound."

She stood trying to decipher what he said. "Oh, the commander keeps you in the unit building over the weekend? That must be fun being surrounded by the officers twenty-four hours a day."

"Gggm ... gym."

"Oh, they place you in the gym by yourself?" She waited some time, then felt compelled to ask another probing question. "Deake, on the Monday that night you spoke to me, I had gotten into a fight with Boris."

"Wwa ... wa ... wwatch."

She paused. "You watched me fighting?" Helena had a sudden thought that the incident might have been the true reason he came out to speak with her. "You said earlier you had a fight. If I mentioned the names, would you tell me if that person is the one you fought? Boris? Satch? Shemp?" she asked as he grunted in agreement. She figured that it had been all of them.

"P ... P ... Pierre."

"All of them jumped you, including Pierre?"

Deake slowly spoke, "Bynn ... now ... Deake ... ss ... sleep."

Helena, left still wondering, gently spoke, "Goodnight, Deake. Hope to see you on Monday."

It was morning as Helena stood by the holding gate. She watched as Boris' master picked him and Shemp up. Torchy stood by her until his master came. She ran up to greet him, rubbing him briskly and telling him how much she'd miss him.

"See you, Helena," he said as he eagerly jogged off. "Have a great weekend!"

"You too, Torchy." Helena smiled, seeing the two off as though they were made for each other.

Satch left next as his master, driving a four-wheel drive truck, pulled up to the front, never getting out from behind the wheel. He simply opened the passenger door and waited. Satch, with slow, ginger steps, walked to the truck and climbed in.

Astonishing her, Champ walked up from behind. "Goodbye, Helena. Enjoy your weekend."

He then walked onto the front step and stood poised, not flinching a muscle, waiting. His master pulled up in a jeep. He jumped out wearing camouflage fatigues, a US Marine's T-shirt with a fighting bulldog plastered on front, and sunglasses and ordered, "Champ, heel one."

Champ stood up straighter, not moving an inch.

"Champ, come."

Champ walked with militarily disciplined steps, high and straight toward his master, then methodically sat in front of him. His master reached out his hand, petting him on the head exactly twice, then questioned, "How is my killer?" while opening the door.

Champ didn't move until his master said, "Jump!"

Champ's master closed the door and they took off.

Seeing Pierre sitting alone, Helena walked over to him. He hesitated to say anything to her until she spoke first. "Hope you have a nice weekend."

"Yeah, you too." He was barely able to speak. Helen decided to walk back over to her spot to wait on her ride. Pierre, for a time looking at her standing alone, decided to drag himself over.

He already figured she had heard a rendition of Deake's story from the other dogs. He defensively explained, "You don't understand. See, at one time, we all shared the same yard, Boris, Deake, Satch, and Shemp. I was the new kid on the block. Deake stayed inside the yard, but even before his master died, he still mainly kept to himself. Of course, the guys would always pick on him, but he would pay it no mind. They picked on me also. Old Deake would speak to me now and then. Did you know he and his master have two plaques displayed on the walls of the canine unit? You didn't see it, huh? At that time, he was labeled the best tracker in the business. Ha-ha, even gave me a few tips. That was until that day."

"What day?" she inquired.

"The day his master was killed. I still remember that day. It was raining hard. Deake, a dog from a suburban city, and I were tracking a sniper who had shot and killed four people over the course of three days. Me and the other dog were on his trail, having sniffed his hat that he dropped, but due to the rain, we, and our masters, lost his escape trail within a few blocks—but not old Deake. He trailed that sniper like he smelled raw sewage on a clear fresh day. Trailed him close to a mile in the rain and tracked him up into an apartment building. As he and his master got in the door, the sniper shot and killed Deake's master instantly. Deake wasn't the same. But then what happened next—I could be judging wrong—but I think it's worse."

"Yes, what is it?"

Looking up to see a passing car, Pierre thought it to be his master. "Well, it was two days after his master's funeral. I still feel guilt."

Pierre paused, not wanting to speak, but then forcing himself to continue, said, "Two days. Boris confronted Deake about his master dying. Badgering him, telling him he was partially to blame. They had a brutal fight. Deake busted Boris up pretty good until Boris's "dogs" jumped in and helped him. They chewed, gashed, and tore into poor old Deake, and I stood by. There was nothing I could do. I was young then."

A tear appeared in Pierre's eye. "I wished I could've done something. It was Boris's idea to have the dogs force me to bite Deake, or else they would to do me like Deake, but worse! I looked at Deake, his eyes. He was badly beaten. He couldn't speak. He couldn't move, but his eyes followed me. His eyes were calling out for help. He watched me as they made me take a nip at him.

"After that, the vet treated him for a week or two. His mouth alone was so badly damaged they had to stitch it with over a hundred stitches. He didn't speak to anyone, wasn't seen much by anybody for two and a half years. Now, only the commander, an old pal of his ex-master, looks after him."

Pierre, looking up, said, "I think your ride is here."

Helena looked up, startled to see her master approaching the front walk.

"Oh, thanks." Starting off, she stopped near him. "Pierre, hey, you shouldn't feel so bad for what you did. You were young and afraid. I'm sure you and Deake can come to some type of understanding."

"No, Helena, I did worse than physically hurt him. I've dishonored him."

"Come on, Helena, let's go home. You ready to go home?" Winston asked.

Helena spoke, "See you on Monday, Pierre." Then off she ran to the open arms of her master.

"Well, my girl, heard you've been in a nasty scrape, huh? Let me take a look." Surveying the various wounded areas, he said, "Oh goodness, Gloria's not going to be too thrilled over this!"

As the two went home, Winston talked as he drove. "I've got a hunch where that Slasher could possibly be. My boss thinks otherwise, but it just boils down to a matter of timing. You know what I mean, girl? My boss says he's within the residential area, but I got a hunch he's off near that park. Near those abandoned buildings somewhere. I can feel it."

That night, Helena stretched out on the living room floor and overheard her master and Gloria having a discussion.

"Honey, I tell you, I'm close. I'm just that close to catching this guy."

"Yes, I believe you and it scares me. Why don't you give it up, quit your job, and go back to being a substitute teacher? The job is just too dangerous—"

"Oh, Gloria, there you go—"

"And another thing, I feel our Helena shouldn't go through such abuse. I'd be just as happy having her as our own personal guard dog, here with a loving family, than being there at that canine unit, training to be a killer!"

"Gloria, dear, you're overreacting."

Their disagreement continued through the night.

* * *

On Monday, fresh upon returning to the canine unit, Helena was confused, seeing the trainers and officers scurrying around in a huff. Torchy was the first to tell her what was going on.

"Hurry, hurry we're supposed to go to the site to assist while Pierre sniffs the area of the Slasher's seventh victim."

Helena, watching as the trainer began loading the dogs into the van, felt a twitch of nervousness. A trainer yelled to them as they ran over to board the van. Pierre was sitting in the front seat with one of the trainers.

"Pierre," the trainer said as he petted the dog. "Come on, today we're gonna show these people what you can do. Do you feel lucky today, boy? Yeah, we'll show them!"

As they all got out of the van—following, scenting, tracking—much to Helena's amazement, Pierre came close to the familiar spot her master had pointed out Friday on their homeward trip.

That night, Helena confessed her fears about her first outing as a police dog in training to Deake.

Deake patiently listened to every word; however, a light, almost familiar scent dabbled at his senses. It was probably undetectable to the average dog, but with his keen sense of smell, his nose pinpointed and deduced that it originated from some principal focal point on Helena's body.

" ... But like I said, Pierre lost the trail after eight blocks," Helena continued.

"R ... r ... range ... li ... li ... lim ... limited."

"Are you saying that his range is limited? But they had another hound there from the Melvindale Police Department; he was some kind of Australian hound."

"M ... Ma ... Maxi ... g ... gggoodd ... bbbut ... rrrange ... limmmti ... ted."

"You're saying his range was limited too, but I don't understand, Deake."

Deake, taking a breath now said, "Ma ... maannny ... ssscents ... cccan't ... ssooort ... ttrue ... ssscent."

You're saying there are too many scents and they are confusing them and making it hard for them to lock on to the true scent." She paused, thinking, and then asked. "Could you sort out the scents, Deake?"

"P . . . ppprobably . . ."

"Listen, Deake, they have an outer shirt and a used piece of tissue belonging to the Slasher. They found them at the site, and now they're inside the compound labeled as evidence. They are supposed to have it out tomorrow so Pierre can have a sniff and go again in the general area. The rest of us are to go off base for additional training. Do you think maybe you could take a whiff of it? I heard of your awards and of you being labeled the best nose in the country."

Deake, quick to cut her off, said, "Deake old . . . qqquit."

"Deake, you've got to be crazy. How could you give up with such a special talent as yours? Can't you see that hundreds of dogs would give up a three-year supply of their best steak bones for the gift that you have? You can't just stand by while all those innocent people and your comrades need your valuable services. Just think of the future victims waiting to be slain by this unknown maniac or even one of us getting hurt trying to improperly track him down. Deake? Deake, are you listening? Deake?"

Deake, wanting to hear no more, stood firm on his decision. Two years ago, he'd considered himself retired and vowed to shirk all police duties. He'd figured that after apprehending 139 felony gunmen, 37 murderers, and somewhere around 56 rapists—and with 17 children found and his long-time loving master dead—he had earned retirement this time.

"Deake, I know you heard me. Say something, please."

"Deake . . . sssleep."

Helena was, to say the least, very disheartened.

In the morning, all the dogs, including Helena, went out and weren't to return until afternoon. Pierre stayed at the base, training in his search-and-smell technique using the evidence. Deake, sitting in his doghouse on this bright, sunshiny day, observed Pierre's technique closely through the peephole in his doghouse, where he had a view of practically everything going down within the yard.

After the outing, the dogs were all winded and eager to be in their kennels. The van entered the outer gate, and as the dogs climbed out, an unusual sight caught Satch's attention.

"Lookit! Lookit that in the field!"

Boris, taking a gander along the fence, remarked, "I don't believe it. It's the freak, Deake!"

"Deake the freak!"

Helena, still in the van, heard the dogs clamoring with laughter.

"Look at that big gumpy palooka, he never looked bigger," Boris said.

"He looks like a clown; his ears are gonna flap away," Shemp laughed.

The two trainers, along with the commander, were surprised at Deake's appearance in the yard as well, because in the past he had been about as active as a rock. They tossed around his favorite ball, and he ran galloping awkwardly after it. His commander friend was pleased to see him up and about.

As Deake ran, his huge, sloping jaws practically touched the ground with each forward motion, while his ears, catching even the lightest of breezes, fanned up into the air like a whirlybird. Trying to pick up the ball with his massive jaws provided another laugh for the group as Deake lacked any finesse, dropping the ball out of his mouth every time he attempted to retrieve it.

Helena, now exiting the van to the chant of "Deake the freak," looked curiously toward the field and became breathless at such a revolting sight. She actually considered it harsh to the eyes.

Boris suggested, "Hey, Shemp, why don't you go snatch the ball from him?"

Torchy, now alongside Helena, said, "Well, so that's the renowned Deake, huh? He's a big old fella. Wow! Look at him go!"

Helena, astonished at his appearance, questioned, "Torchy, why does his face hang like that? And those large floppy ears. My goodness it's like someone's idea of a bad joke or something!"

"I must admit he does look—putting it mildly—different. Truthfully, he's downright unpleasing to anyone's eye, but he's a bloodhound. What did you expect?"

While the rest of the dogs went inside the fence, Helena was left standing there, still in shock. Shemp stole the ball from Deake's fetch game. Deake tried to chase after him and looked as if he was in a crawl while Shemp ran circles around him. Deake reached Shemp, tripped up over his own jaws, rolled over into a doofus fall, and awkwardly got up, causing the dogs to howl with laughter, which brought them to the ground.

Deake, scenting Helena, turned around, then lopsidedly ran toward her with his off-balance gallop. Helena, seeing him approach, found herself unknowingly backing up, as if to run as he got closer.

"Hihehehele . . . na."

Helena barely spoke an audible greeting as she looked upon his three-sizes-too-long floppy ears and the droopy, sagging mouth, which appeared to have surplus rows of unending flesh. His mouth drooled bucket loads of saliva. His eyes appeared droopy and looked solemn and sad. Now, feeling embarrassed, she couldn't bear to look upon his face.

Torchy stood near Helena, having waited for an introduction by Helena, informally introduced himself.

Deake noticing Helena's bizarre behavior, asked, "HeHeHelena iss something errww—wrong?"

Helena, with her eyes closed and head turned, cringed. "No, Deake."

Deake walked closer and clumsily brushing against her. Helena let out an unpleasant whimper in hopes that he wouldn't touch her.

"Come on, Deake, bring back the ball, boy," the commander cried out.

Deake, hurt, drew his huge head closer to Helena's tiny one, but she retracted, refusing to move toward him. He sniffed her, ran at full speed back toward the commander, then went past him into the security of his doghouse.

"What's gotten into him?" the commander questioned.

The other dogs laughed raucously at such an embarrassing sight.

"Well, that was a downright insensitive display," Torchy commented to Helena.

With tears in her eyes, she replied, "I've never seen anything like him before in my life. I was so—stunned."

The dogs walked to their kennels for rest. That afternoon, as the commander was on his way home, he stopped in and looked into Deake's doghouse. Crouching, the commander said, "Hey there, old Deake boy. You gave us all a pleasant shock out there seeing you like the old days when our pal Ralphie was around. Ha, ha, I bet you remember those days well too!" Rubbing Deake, he continued. "Well truthfully, I miss him too. You know, you being out there, I thought that was our ray of hope. You'd give us that edge you and Ralphie were famous for. You know we need you, pal—bad. I can't help but to think that if Ralphie were still alive today, he'd be right on that Slasher's heels by now." Bringing his hand from behind his back, he placed an old police cap in the shadows. "Here you are, boy. I been meaning to give you that for some time now. On the inside of the hat, as you can see, it's got yours and Ralphie's picture for those string of triple homicide arrests you both pulled down." With a final pet, the "salty old dog" who himself, remembered the golden times of yesteryear, departed.

Deake, looking carefully at the cap, sniffed it, and then in misery softly rested his head upon it.

Helena, after talking with both Torchy and Pierre, returned to her doghouse. She noticed a difference about it. Taking a closer look, she saw that the house had been rearranged to its original spot. She tried smoothing things over with a heart-felt apology, but her every attempt failed. Deake, clinging to his emotional hurt, ignored her every word. The following night Helena, hopeful still, merely just wished him a goodnight.

* * *

The following day an unexpected tragedy occurred, and Helena's entire world collapsed around her. Winston suddenly went missing. After he failed to report back to his bureau or home, the police department scoured the city looking for him.

Helena was distressed as her unit was mobilized to make a search of large areas but uncovered nothing. An agonizing week passed without a single clue, and Helena remained at the compound over the weekend. Through her pain and misery, she couldn't help but feel even more terrible for Gloria and the kids. It troubled her knowing Gloria was probably up all night in erratic fits of tears. Sitting in the kennel over those two nights, Helena had never felt so alone.

The next Monday, Helena stayed silently in her kennel, not leaving it once. The following day, she noticed something peculiar about the yard. Not a dog was out. She found this strange and began thinking that something was wrong or maybe that there had been a breaking development. She tiptoed the length of one side of the yard, carefully noticing that Torchy and Pierre were still sleeping soundly in their kennels. Boris and his group hid smugly behind the compound, watching her every move, while a singularly watchful eye from a peephole observed them.

Boris, looking over to Champ, whispered, "Okay, kid, get ready."

Helena, taken off guard, was astonished and then overwhelmed as Boris's group knocked her to the ground—Satch and Shemp bit into her, forcing then pinning her front half to the ground. Pierre and Torchy, hearing the commotion, immediately awoke.

As Torchy ran towards them, he heard Boris speaking to Champ.

"All right Champ, old boy," Boris exclaimed, while the other two dogs grew more aggressive seeing Boris's pleasure at hearing Helena's screams, "it's your time!"

"What are you stupid idiots doing?" Torchy growled.

"None of your business, boy, so why don't you find some of your own," Boris snarled, jumping quickly to force him to the ground.

"Come on, kid, ain't got all day," Satch yelled.

"Don't do it, Champ. Don't let them sway you into such a stupid act as this!" Torchy pleaded.

Boris nipped him. "I says shut up!"

"Boris, you madman! Stop this! I never thought you'd stoop this low to commit such an appalling act!" Pierre stepped forth to protest.

Shemp walked over as Satch tightened his grip on Helena. "You can zip it, Pierre. This is Champ's first time. Now we wouldn't want to deprive him of his first time. Even you smell it— nature's calling upon her to do her duty."

"Besides, even though she acts like she don't want it, deep down inside she likes it—all your female types do," Boris commented.

Pierre steadily edged his way toward Helena as Boris gave his small-minded speech and jumped suddenly at Satch to gain Helena her freedom, but Shemp, uncovering his ploy, intercepted Pierre's charge and they bitterly engaged in battle.

Boris shouted over the ensuing conflict, "Go ahead, lad, nothing'll stop you now. Remember how you said she looked at you in the academy. She good as wants it!"

Champ, slowly advancing, couldn't block the pleas of Helena or the shouts of Torchy out of his mind. Suddenly, the ground shook underneath them as a huge body collided with and bowled over everyone in its path. Rising up, Deake faced Boris again.

Boris was in utter shock as the heavy-jawed gargantuan looked defiantly down at him. There was the sound only of a quiet breeze.

"HHHeleeenaa . . . ggo . . . beyond ffffenccccce qqqquickly," Deake advised.

Boris's dogs began to snarl their disapproval.

Pierre swiftly took a stand at Torchy's side. "Go quickly you two. Make your break. Me and Torchy can hold off these three old windbags!"

Deake joined Helena, and running in a full gallop, they daringly crossed the street and went down the block as the alerted trainers called out to them.

The night progressed and they found refuge in a back alley. Neither of them said much until Deake hopped up. "Ccccome on."

Helena, still depressed, simply followed with her head hanging. Stopping in the rear of a building, which read "Blues Note Jazz Bar," Deake sifted through the garbage, sampling the leftovers. Looking over to Helena he said, "Use to rrrunn heere . . . tttime ago"

Helena watched as Deake shifted food her way. "Ssssoulll foffofood gggood!

Helena was now quite hungry and took a sniff. Although not used to table scraps, the smell alleviated her trepidations, for they had the same tasty aroma as the food Gloria prepared for her master. She sampled it without much choice and loved the flavor. Gobbling it up, she felt deprived and foolish for not having tried scraps before when Winston or the kids tried dishing some to her underneath the table before dessert.

Looking over at Deake as he laid his massive body amidst the comfort of the trash, his huge jaws chomping away merrily as he savored the appetizing food, she temporarily forgot her worries, thinking the sight was, in a sense, unusually comical. She let out a lighthearted chuckle.

Deake, who was entranced by the smooth sounds of the sax player playing nearby, turned around and questioned, "Wwhatttz... amatter?"

Seeing that he had corn bread and black-eyed peas pasted to and dangling from his mouth caused Helena to laugh harder. "You, Deake. You look so funny. You know you're a mess!"

She walked over and licked the food residue off him. Deake, finding humor in himself, laughed. Helena, tickled to hear such a goofy laugh, laughed louder.

Later during the course of the evening, Helena found herself lying next to him, enjoying the sound of a cool trumpet blowing jazz over the air, the picturesque scenery of the back alley, and the sight of a half-moon shining in the backdrop. After a while of peaceful, somber meditation, she advised, "It's late, Deake. We'd better be heading back."

"Aafff ... afafte rtthis wewe ... hunt."

Helena, surprised, asked, "Deake, you don't really mean—"

"Deake ... knnnowss ... De—ake ... underrr ... standss."

She was so surprised and elated that she kissed him.

Deake raised his massive body up. "Snsnsniffed sscscents ... weekend llllllong innn ccommpound."

She was now overwhelmed with surprise.

"Tthththought it ouout ... weee mmmumumust go nnno now!"

As Deake trekked off, Helena called out to him, "Wait, Deake!" Deake returned, looking puzzled. "The jazz is still playing. Let's not leave just yet. Can we lie here listening for a short while?"

Deake's mind was already made up. He was geared toward working, but looking into her beautiful, pleading eyes, he couldn't refuse. He graciously granted her request.

Awhile later, there was a rustling at Gloria's door. Gloria, still awake, Investigated the noise. Feeling somewhat joyful, she smiled, opening the door. "It's Helena! Why, what are you doing here, girl, at this early hour of the morning?"

Helena rubbed against Gloria with concern and brushed by her.

Gloria backed up, looking into the eyes of the huge lumbering figure before her. "And she brought—a friend?"

The kids ran into the room. "Mommy, Mommy, has Daddy returned? Is it Daddy?"

They were surprised to see Helena and immediately began rubbing her as she licked them both. But, remembering the task at hand, Helena began to search methodically around the room.

Gloria said to Helena, "You're acting strange. What's going on here?"

Helena looked around further while Gloria, confused by her behavior, followed. The kids then noticed Deake.

As Helena rushed toward the utility room, she teasingly quipped to Deake over her shoulder, "Hope you like kids, my dear."

The children were laughing with excitement as Chris hid underneath one of Deake's big floppy ears while Terri hung from the other like a rope.

"Ittsss...alllllrighhht."

Helena dragged back a pair of pants, holding them to Deake's nose. He sniffed. "Gggoodd, bbu-but dededeeterrrgentss."

Gloria, watching the strange phenomenon, finally caught on and hurriedly ran down to the basement. The children followed, insistently questioning what was going on. Gloria realized that Helena's friend was a bloodhound and had a chance at picking up her husband's scent better than anyone or anything. She frantically searched in the dirty clothes hamper and pulled out a pair of Winston's sweatpants. She rushed back upstairs, ecstatic, hopeful, and thankful all at the same time. She presented the pants to Helena.

Deake sniffed at them and carried them off in his mouth. Helena wagged her tail as they headed to the door. Gloria called them back, hugging them both. "Please, find my Winston—please. I beg of you. We do miss him so—he's all we've got."

"Mommy, Mommy, why are you crying?" Chris asked.

Terri began crying, seeing her mother cry as Gloria watched the dogs depart.

Helena took Deake to the exact spots they had searched and where Pierre left off, then pointed to her master's own suspicions of where the Slasher might be. They both continued searching through the night and into midmorning. Helena, growing weary, lay down to momentarily rest.

"Ccccome ... nooo tititime!" Deake said, nudging her back up. He began sniffing about again in a synchronized, sweeping-plot motion using a panning method to detect every traceable scent. This was time consuming and confusing at times, but he knew the longer he kept at it, the greater were his chances of catching on to a lead scent.

Helena was pooped after still searching into the late afternoon. Deake left her to rest, since she had had no sleep all night or the previous day. Deake's search continued through the night well into the following day. During the following afternoon, Helena rested, waiting impatiently for Deake and feeling that hope was dwindling with every minute. Deake's sudden flopping around startled her.

"Ffffoound... lleeleelead..scent! Huhuhurhurry!"

Helena followed him excitedly through the city streets until they came upon a grassy abandoned field where Deake uncovered a cigarette wrapper. The Slasher had possibly held it in his pocket over time then discarded it after use.

"Hhhhhere!"

Helena looking about, "Hey, we're here?"

Deake sniffed around a wider circumference as he picked up more scattered traces.

"How long ago? Which way? Is he still alive?"

Deake didn't answer, but continued sniffing. "Ffffollow."

Deake followed a trail only to lose it. Returning back to his point of origin, he followed it again only to lose it again. He painstakingly followed his footsteps back. This kept on into the night.

Helena grew tired from watching him and was overcome with sleep. Figuring she'd close her eyes and snooze for a few minutes, she instead dozed off. Her peaceful dream of being home again with her master and family was abruptly ended by slobbery licks from Deake.

At first, she was angry at being awakened from such a pleasant dream, but then she smiled, looking at Deake's cheerful face. "What is it?" she asked.

"Llooook... bbebeaubeautiful."

She smiled again.

"Fffounnd ... plllace ... fffolllow."

Helena immediately jumped up. "Where? Why didn't you tell me? Is he okay? You sure you found it? What makes you think so? Can't you run any faster?"

Deake had earlier followed the leading scent up to a demolition site. The property to be demolished was a high-rise apartment building. The wrecking ball had already demolished the rear of the structure.

Helena, looking up, spoke, "This makes good sense. Who in their right mind would want to risk their life searching this death trap?"

They both slipped between the cracks of a boarded-up divider fence. Walking through the rear opening of the building, they climbed to the hallway of the second floor where Deake walked inside an open, gutted room. He pointed an open soup can and a balled-up wax cracker package out to her.

"Deake, they were here. You think they are probably further up?"

Deake, looking around, remembered to have patience with her, since this was only her second case. "Sshshshshhhhh!"

He picked up two strong scents, matching Winston and the Slasher. Tracking a route up the stairs, they climbed over fallen debris and garbage. Deake muttered, "Cacacacau. . . tion." The upper-level stairs were damaged and exposed by the wrecking ball, and there were no guardrails.

As Helena and Deake were making their careful climb, inside a seventeenth-floor apartment Winston lay on the floor, weak from not having eaten for days. He was bound from behind and gagged. His captor stood peeping out the seventeenth-floor window, holding Winston's gun in his hand, while the captor's knife was stashed in a pouch on his side.

"That letter should've made it to them by now. They should've given a sign or something. All I'm asking for is three million in small untraceable bills so that I can start a new life over in Canada, right across the river. Yes sir, Mr. Policeman, buddy of mine got this small boat. All I gotta do is pay him a thousand and he'll boat me there smooth, simple, and no customs. What was that? Did you hear that, Mr. Policeman?"

Winston's eyes shifted, as his edgy captor got startled every time the wind blew. Winston knew that the situation was bad and he had to escape. He knew that anytime a captor told you his method of escape and there was ransom money involved, there was a nine out of ten chance he was going to kill you to leave no loose ends. Winston had an ace up his sleeve, though, and had his own plan. His kidnapper didn't know he was double-jointed and considerably limber for his age. That's one thing he contributed to his job, having to keep physically fit. He knew he'd have to get his hands quickly in front of him and rush the Slasher instantly to wrestle the gun from him. Trying to outrun his captor wouldn't help because he was physically unbalanced and chancing those stairs in his weakened condition would be suicidal. Another disadvantage was that he didn't know his way around. Whatever the effort, Winston knew he had to do it and do it soon, for a reply to the Slasher's letter would be sent shortly and in his mind, no matter what the response, he knew the end result for him would be fatal.

Deake and Helena, now in the sixteenth-floor stairwell, heard noise from an apartment on the seventeenth floor. They proceeded cautiously as they lightly stepped onto the floor, both edging towards the sounds of the room. Then Deake stopped.

Helena whispered, "He's there. I smell him. We've found him, Deake!"

Deake wanted her to be strong and ready, for he knew from past experience that just because a dog uncovered a human scent, it didn't necessarily mean it would be a live scent.

"Rerereremember . . . bebebeyonnnnd dooorbe bebee pre-eppppapared!"

They both stood ready at the door. Helena managed to utter a quick prayer.

"Rats, those rats are everywhere making noises," the Slasher yelled to himself.

Suddenly, Helena and Deake burst inside like a flash. Deake surprised the Slasher, knocking him over as the gun fell. Deake handled the Slasher with ease as Helena backed off to check on Winston's condition. As she pranced around him eagerly, he tried to place his hands in front of him. Deake attacked the man, pinning the Slasher underneath himself and had him under control. Deake took a mere second to check Helena's condition but didn't check the location of the gun, which had fallen underneath his and the Slasher's bodies. The Slasher, seemingly without movement, had slid the gun back into his hand during the quick-paced excitement. He fired it twice into Deake's chest cavity and Deake screamed, feeling lead pierce clean through his body.

Helena watched in disbelief as Deake lost his footing and fell backwards, crashing heavily against the windowsill. Loud thunder erupted again as the Slasher pumped off another two rounds into poor Deake. His body crashed out the broken window and plummeted seventeen stories. Helena, furious, sprung at the gunman before he could aim at her. Charging him with a vengeance, just like in training, she grabbed his gun hand, shaking it ferociously and jarring the weapon loose.

Winston, with his arms now in front of him leapt like no tomorrow for his fallen gun. Helena lost herself in her attack and pierced her fangs deeply into the Slasher's arm while he, unnoticed, unsnapped his knife pouch. Brandishing the knife, which he poised in a downward striking position, he yelled, "Call it off!"

Winston, having a fix on him, ordered, "Drop your weapon first! NOW!"

Helena continuously yanked the Slasher's arm, viciously overwrought with anger; she was unaware of the deadly knife looming over her head. The Slasher looked at Winston, smiling, then in one quick stroke, Helena screeched. Winston fired his gun until it emptied. Helena lay bleeding as Winston sat by her side attempting first aid.

Time passed.

Helena's condition was listed by the veterinarian as guarded.

The days turned into weeks that passed slowly, and she dreamt only of Deake, her love. She believed him still alive. She thought of their long night talks, of his shy, kind demeanor. His gentle heart, his warm expressive eyes, and his looks that she now admired. She dreamed of his relentless dedication to his call to duty, his valiant rescue of her from Boris's gang, and their first date—that magical endless night she shared alone with him. The department, no longer able to foot the long-term care bill, had to rely upon a collection to be taken in Helena's name for her continued medical treatment. The commander himself made a hefty contribution.

Four months quickly passed. Helena, to everyone's surprise, had three pups: two boys and one girl. Two days later, she died, succumbing to her wounds and complications during birth.

Winston's family mourned the loss of Helena and Deake and honored two of the pups with their parents' names.

The commander, as his last decree before retirement, placed a posthumous plaque for both dogs in the canine unit hallway and further inducted all three pups, by special consent of the family, of course, into the unit when they become of age. The canine unit gang couldn't wait for their arrival and welcomed them with open arms—even Boris, who had suddenly had a change of heart.

No pair could be happier, however, than Deake and Helena, who were now together, sharing forever.

* * *

Brian, moved, caught his breath. "Divine Spirit, how can two—overcoming such odds—display such courage, find a first love, and be taken from that realm so quickly? It saddens me to know such courage and love as they shared is now inaccessible in a world that's in dire need of such."

"True, little one, but courage, like a flower, grows renewed like the passing of the seasons, and luckily it isn't restricted to one bound by the duty of the badge,"

Ramrod

An apprehensive tension filled the air as droves of people waited upon the gate; they held on to lucky mementos, chanted in false prayer, or nervously twitched a body appendage in hopes of attaining "the big one." The race chiseled away, inch by inch, so many of their dreams and savings, while the very lives of those held behind the gate would be determined by just this one heat.

Suddenly, the harsh clanging of the bell—*Stand ready*—the hurrying zing of the electronic rabbit departing in the breeze—*There it goes*—the gates opening—*After it! Run for your life!*

"They're off!"

Ramrod (his name given to him by a stable cleaner) stood leashed and watched with much interest while the dogs zipped by him in a blur. A young greyhound of six months and still in training, he watched his mother, Liberian Queen, running in this heat. He observed the human crowd's usual reactions and behaviors as the dogs approached the finish gate. As the race closed, the trainer tugged at him. "Come on, Ramrod, stop daydreaming. You're not born to think, you know!"

As the trainer lead him around near the finish line, Ramrod observed the winner, Donna Sees Red, being superficially petted by her distinguished owner, an elderly, refined, blue-blooded gentleman. He was dressed in a conservative black suit and a crisp white shirt with gold cuff links, two gold rings adorning both white, freshly manicured hands. The lightest scent of gentle aromatic cologne hovered in his air space. He topped off his dapper attire with an expensive topcoat—which seemed to repel every speck of dirt that drifted toward it—and an elegantly dressed, energetic, overly enthusiastic young lady, who seemed out of place in her surroundings, despite her exquisite façade.

"Is it okay to pet him? Is it?" she asked.

The gentleman politely ignored his guest and talked over her to his team of dog handlers as if she were transparent. "She is still receiving the DRAA's minimum requirement dosage for pain, right?"

"Of course, Mr. Leeds."

"We're steady on our injections for the "other" vitamins, are we, gentlemen?"

"You bet, sir!"

"Precisely, gentlemen. That's the reason you are paid and paid well. I'm sure all present parties wish to be continuously so rewarded?"

"Yes, sir!"

He smiled smugly, and turning to his near-invisible companion he said, "Darcy, darling, what was it you said?"

Ramrod looked about at the other dogs that were being rubbed down, washed down, or inspected for wear. He observed near the rear of the line one of the masters yelling high-blown obscenities and brutally whipping his dog with a leash as the dog crumpled at his feet and curled into itself like a little quivering ball. Another owner, who appeared to be dismayed, handed the rein of his leashed dog over to another human. Ramrod, although young and still training, took in all these sights and images.

Long after practice, he sat in the kennel stable alongside his mother while she talked with him as she did every night. She was a beautifully sculpted animal, paramount in aerodynamic design. Typifying a surgically crafted, muscular, lean-cut shape, she had a coal black coat with a small, distinctive diamond patch of white fur on her forehead, which earned her the name Queen.

"That's the whole key inside the gate—trying to stay focused. Many dogs have lost the race of catching the white rabbit even before the gate opened because they refused to concentrate. They let the fear of the crowd, the claustrophobic panic due to the closing of the gate behind them, the uncertainty of the dogs barking around them, and the tension of wanting and needing to outperform their competitors get to them. All this pressure stifles them before the starting gates open and then it's over before it begins. Ramrod, are you listening to me, Son?"

Ramrod's head jerked forward now, his large bright eyes focused only on his mother. "Yes, Mom."

"Son, I'm trying to educate you about the race of catching the white rabbit so at least you'll have a chance. You're the only child they've let me keep. Your three sisters and two brothers were taken away. I only pray that they were auctioned or sold off somewhere or given a good decent home. I hope that they didn't suffer tragic consequences like the others."

Her mind began to drift as she thought of the other litters that she had had. She thought about the status of the other race dogs in the past.

Ramrod watched his mother while she was in muted thought, then finally asked, "Mother, what is the purpose for that white canvas truck out back?"

Breaking her train of thought, Queen answered, "Don't be concerned with that. Don't you see I'm trying to prepare you so you can do well? From the small number of times I've gotten a chance to see you run, I've noticed you've got one of the best takeoffs from the starting gate. Now, if I could teach you to build that asset, you stand a good chance of winning some races, which would get you some notoriety where you'll run a strong possibility of being adopted by a well-to-do fan or race board member and find a good home."

"But Mom, what happened to Tea Biscuit, Dark Velvet, and Sapphire Blue? Did they catch the white rabbit? Did they go to good homes?"

"Ramrod, see, you're always thinking rather than listening. You remind me so of your father. Don't be concerned with them. Keep your mind focused. Your only concern is to care for yourself!" She stepped closer and looked into her son's eyes. "Son, I'm telling you this for a reason. Tomorrow will be your first race and I want you to do well, if not win. My time with you may be short, Son, because even though I've made a somewhat strong showing with younger dogs, I've placed a distant fifth overall. I know from past experience with other dogs that I'm going to have to do exceptionally well over the next few days, at least show a strong fourth or above, because investors are losing money on me. It's funny—"

She drifted again. "I can remember a year ago. I was always the odds-on favorite. I was hot and they made big money on me. Now there's been talk of retiring me. I haven't heard anything of being adopted. I guess a bad fate would be sending me on to the circuit, or even worse, the breeding farms," she said as she stood. She had another frightening thought, but she didn't want to mention her last possible fate. She didn't want to re-stir her son's inquisitive and imaginative pot by uttering a word about the white canvas truck.

"Mom, do you mean—?"

She became serious and spoke tersely. "Son, don't question me, just listen to what I've told you. Take it in and etch it in stone somewhere in that brilliant mind of yours. This is your chance. Those few brief moments of chasing that white rabbit will put you in a spotlight—a spotlight where only a chosen few can breathe an easier life. Do you hear me, Son?"

"Okay, Mom, don't worry. I'll catch that white rabbit just for you."

She smiled, losing her brief moment of hostility, then caressingly nudged up against him.

The next day the huge metal door clanged shut at the starting gate behind him. Looking around, he noticed some dogs barked and howled while others stayed poised and calm and didn't make a sound. Remembering what his mother said and knowing she would watch his first race, Ramrod stood focused.

"I need that white rabbit," one of the dogs yelled.

"I'll catch her quicker than any of you —"

"Just stand out of my way! The white rabbit is mine!"

Glancing slightly behind him to his right through a small peephole, Ramrod could see his mother a ways off, training and preparing for her forthcoming heat. She trained, keeping a guarded eye on the track for her son.

Ramrod jumped at the thunderous sound of the gates closing after more dogs were ushered into the starting gate. The noise level grew with the introduction of more dogs. Looking around again, he noticed the more experienced dogs were quiet and well focused. Blocking out all the sounds, Ramrod channeled his thoughts, trying to focus his mind. For him, everything seemingly sputtered and gradually slowed to a near freeze-frame pace.

White rabbit—I mus—

Hearts quickened, breaths became dry. Suddenly, the familiar short burst of the on-line ready sounded as the electronic gates jerked in a nervous twitch and clanged in a successful test, clear, on, and fully functional. *STAND READY* the on-line ready bell chimed. For the dogs, all motion ceased except for their thumping hearts and the inescapable ringing in their ears. *GET SET, there it goes!*

The white rabbit! No! Keep focused, keep focused! Ramrod's heart felt like it stopped; his muscles tightened up—frozen. He stood with all his might, trying to prevent his body from falling over. His whole body felt like compacted lead.

He knew there was only one way to overcome this weighed feeling, the steady ringing of the electronic bell—*THIS IS IT!* his mind shouted.

The gates sliced open, and he burst into a flying sprint. After a few yards, he looked ahead and saw nothing but the white rabbit some distance ahead, and the only sounds he heard were the thousand thundering paws behind him.

Making the first turn, he found he was still alone. The white rabbit had increased its lead, though. Passing a grandstand, he heard a cheering crowd. Turning another bend, he suddenly felt another dog, along his side just behind him, pacing him. A few yards more, and two other dogs were close at his heels. Turning another bend, he watched as the white rabbit's lead increased even further.

Ramrod decided to pour on the speed as one of the dogs that had remained focused at the starting gate moved from behind him and now ran just slightly ahead of him. Picking up his stride and rounding a final turn, another of the focused dogs made his move just inside, passing him up. Ramrod picked up the pace and noticed that the thundering paws behind slowly began to lag. It was clearly just the three of them edging towards the rapidly disappearing white rabbit.

Ramrod, now running as hard as he could, regained the lead, his tongue flapping in the breeze as his heart pounded like a hammer trying to burst out of his chest. Unnoticed by him, the crowd began cheering on their feet. The dog on the outside challenged him with a fleeting burst of energy, but Ramrod countered with his own, keeping the dog at a distance. Then from the inside track, the other dog passed him in a well-timed burst, gaining half a lead on him.

Suddenly, pushing himself to his limit, Ramrod felt something inside of him fly loose. It felt like it was banging around inside of him, causing a chain reaction of pain to circulate throughout his entire body. His pace abruptly slowed as his stride shortened. He tried with all his might to correct it, but he failed.

Now the dog on the outside was neck and neck with him as he heard another pounding of paws upon his heels. The white rabbit was out of sight. A few yards more, he crossed the finish line. The other dogs slowed after crossing; however, he continued to run, looking for the white rabbit and wondering to where it had escaped. Members of the audience cheered him on as he eluded several handlers who attempted to stop him.

At the end of the day, his mother lectured him again. "You took a very close third. I'm proud of you, Son, on your first showing. You ran an outstanding race. I feel you really took second. Covered Stock was definitely behind you for most of the race. Son, you had first place. That race alone says a lot about your capabilities. You're a champion runner."

"Yes, Mom, but I didn't catch the white rabbit."

She laughed. "Don't worry about that just yet. In time, you'll catch him, but now you must train to build your endurance for the last quarter of the race. That's your only weakness." She smiled, looking upon his young, disappointed face.

"How'd you do, Mom?"

Without a change of expression, she said, "I came in a close fifth, but tomorrow I'll do better. So let's concentrate on you and your heat tomorrow!" Liberian Queen continued instructing her son throughout the night on various training tips, the habits of his competitors, using the track to his favor, and other helpful hints.

At his next race, Ramrod stood inside the starting gate and looked over to his right. Lined up next to him was Maxi's Clout, an acquaintance he'd only ever said hello to. Alongside Maxi was No Quarter, a friend slightly older than Ramrod was, who had experience in the race game.

"Good luck, Ramrod. If you catch that rabbit before me, I'd like to celebrate with ya."

Looking up nervously over the stalls Ramrod answered, "Sure, No Quarter, you're on."

Looking in his direction alongside of No Quarter was Winsome Winy; she only responded with a smile when their eyes met. Over to his immediate left was the odds-on favorite Blue Jet, who stood positioned in silence. Next over was Erv's Pride, another acquaintance, then Toulon's Masterpiece.

Ramrod, beginning to get into focus, awaited his target—the white rabbit. His trigger? The swift opening of the gates, which transformed him into an exploding, energy–infused, mass-bearing projectile aimed at one goal. The bell sounded. The electronic gates opened to the roar of the crowd in the background.

Later that night he and his mother spoke about his race. "Second! You made second place and I'm proud of you! That Blue Jet beat you out, but he's one of the best, an experienced professional and an accomplished runner who has won many championships—" Ramrod drifted in thought while his mother talked.

He was dismayed still by not having captured the white rabbit. A dog named Dad's Pleasure came in third, Winsome Winy fourth, Maxi's Clout took fifth, while his friend No Quarter took sixth, Erv's Pride seventh, and Toulon's Masterpiece took last.

Ramrod, listening with indifference, pawed non-attentively at the straw and dirt under his feet inside their stable. Looking around into the shadows of the stable, he found a suitable opening in his mother's ongoing rambling marathon to ask a question.

"How'd you do, Mom?"

Breaking her flow of speech for the moment, she stated, "I placed sixth— but I'm so happy about your showing that in tomorrow's race I'm gonna run faster than the wind."

He listened patiently to her lecturing until finally she decided it was time for them both to turn in.

The next day, Ramrod was saddened again by not capturing the white rabbit, even though he took first place. His proud mother took fourth place in her event. Ramrod noticed two new dogs in the lineup. The following day, he captured only second place; his mother took sixth. Today, he noticed another new face. That evening back inside the stable, strangely his mother wasn't herself. She was unusually quiet and guarded and this worried him, driving him right up to the breaking point of asking.

Her muddled response was simply, "Nothing, dear, I'm okay." However, when walking by to rest, a telltale groan forced itself from deep within her body and strained out against the will of her stubborn mouth.

He knew, but couldn't say why, his mother was in pain.

The next day, Ramrod beat out all the dogs for first place. His mother came in last place in her heat.

That evening there wasn't much conversation shared between the two, but as they neared sleep, his mother uttered softly into his overburdened ears, "Dream peaceful. I love you."

The following day, Ramrod was surprised senseless to see his mother aligning herself adjacent to him in the starting gates. He glanced over at her, but she didn't resemble herself. She appeared distant and drunk with pain. Ramrod, quiet at first, turned his head back toward his mother as the stand ready bell alarmed.

"Mom, you're gonna do alright—don't worry. Just run like the wind and I'll follow you."

The buzzer rang. The electronic gates sprung open as the dogs all bounded out of the gate. Liberian Queen, purging her mind of pain, ran strong with her son's encouragement on the straightaway and the first bend. Ramrod ran right behind her, nudging her ahead of the pack. Just around the second bend, pain overwhelmed her senses, slowing her down. Dogs passed her on both sides.

Ramrod took off after them, then looking back to his mother, she urged him, "Go on, leave me! Finish the race!"

She was down to a painful creep. The spectators began to show their disapproval with boos. Ramrod solidly positioned himself in forth position, abandoned the race, and ran back to escort his mother. Flying refuse and other rubbish began pelting the mother and son as he tried coaxing her to run in her agony.

"The track is fixed!" someone shouted.

"I spent $10.00 on this heavy-odds dog, and this is what you amount to? You poor excuse of a dog! They should have you shipped to the soap factory!"

"I betted big money on that Ramrod and look it—this track's fixed. Let's storm the halls of the commission!"

The shouts of discontent continued well after they limped across the finish line.

The night that followed was one of the most uncertain nights he could remember since being a pup. Early the next morning right after chow, Ramrod found himself wandering beyond the rear of the track compound. Up to this point he had been escorted by handlers, but this morning he was aimlessly traveling beyond his normal limit. He walked through a fence, observing never-before-seen sights and hearing a continuous thumping noise. He carefully wandered toward the sound's origin.

"That should do it?" one handler asked.

"Yes, that's the last one for now," another handler answered.

The human voices disappeared into the building. Curiously turning the corner, Ramrod observed a flatbed truck. On the back of the truck lay many dogs; some were his friends who seemed asleep. Resting peacefully, Erv's Pride lay at the top of the pile, quiet and motionless. He lay alongside Toulon's Masterpiece, and two rows underneath them dangled Maxi's Clout.

"Hey, what are you guys doing? Having a group nap session? Why wasn't I invited?" He momentarily awaited a response. Taking a light whiff of the group, he had a sudden uneasy feeling throughout his entire body. Then reluctantly drawing nearer, he said, "Come on, gang, this isn't a very good joke. Somebody say something."

He was suddenly startled by one of the handlers snatching him back.

"What the hell you doing this far from the track—you trying to escape?" he slurred.

As the handler jerked him along back towards the track, another truck—going almost unnoticed, hidden in front of the other truck—echoed with a familiar cry. "Ramrod!" Here! Come here, my son!"

Ramrod broke away from the intoxicated handler. Running beyond the truck, he observed his mother caged and helpless inside a huge truck as dogs around her snarled, howled, or fought. His mother, through the pandemonium about her, looked beaten; her eyes were swollen almost shut from crying and had only a single tear in them as she displayed a contrary smile.

"Mom, what is this? What is going on? Where are you off to?" He heard the closing of the truck's door in front of his mother.

"Ssshhh, Son. I have to go away now."

Tears began forming in his eyes as the truck's engines exploded to life. "What, Mom? What do you mean? I want to go."

"I have a hundred things to tell you!" she shouted, trying to speak over the ruckus of the fighting inside the cage she shared with the fifteen or so other dogs.

"Ramrod, come closer, my son. Quickly! I haven't much time."

Ramrod, moved to within a whisper's shot of his mother as she looked endearingly upon his young, innocent, hurt face.

"Listen, Child, and don't start to go to pieces on me, because there's not enough tears you could shed to get us both out of this predicament. You'll have to cry enough to submerge all seven continents under a sea of water, so you hush that childish sniffling right this second. Be brave, Son. You must be brave. You're an adult now, and I praise the Lord for giving me such a gift as to see one of my own children reach maturity. Son, listen to me—"

The truck began to gear ahead as the driver held his foot to the brake while talking with an attendant.

Ramrod's mother tried to rush every word in her mind—everything she felt she had to tell him—to fit it all into their last few seconds. "I'm leaving for the circuit—"

"Will I see you again, Mom?"

Even knowing they would never see each other again, she still gave him a ray of hope. "There's a chance."

Ramrod held his head down in acceptance, defeated by circumstances beyond his control.

"Hold your head up, Son! You've amazed your mother. You're so smart, the brightest dog I've ever known. Look at me! Look into my eyes!"

He looked into the dark, shadowed confines of the cage only seeing saddened eyes and pearly teeth flashing behind in a hostile fight.

She said, "I haven't much time, so I want you to promise me."

"What?" he mumbled over his sniffling.

"Promise me you'll always remember something."

The man's foot released the brake as the truck coasted off.

"Always remember in this game, please only care for yourself."

The truck accelerated off, as he followed faithfully behind, trying to not lose sight of his mother.

"I love you," she spoke, as two of the handlers caught Ramrod from behind and held his body in a firm grasp.

The truck paused as a guard lazily opened the exterior gate that routed towards the streets. As Ramrod fought to break free of the handlers, the truck hummed away.

"Catch the white rabbit for me, Son."

He ceased struggling to hear her last request, and then she was gone.

* * *

Six months passed. Ramrod's performance, which had seemingly peaked during the first few months of his mother's absence, had dwindled to a mediocre showing. With his spirit hollow with disillusion, he had emphatically given up his quest to capture the white rabbit.

A great number of his friends from his mother's time like No Quarter, Winsome Winy, and others were long gone. He, at times, consulted with new faces and new names like Pawn Takes Queen, Beacon's Point, Dollars Make Sense, Winning Lotto Ticket, and Blinky. The faces and names came and went, yet for the most part, as his mother made him promise, he kept his distance from them.

As evening fell, Ramrod lay in his stable after earlier having showed a comfortable third-place finish in his race. He stretched out amidst the straw covering the floor, his mind half in thought, half in sleep. Hearing a noise at the outer door, he merely lifted his head to observe a handler strangely opening his bin at this unusually late hour of the night. Catching his eye was a smaller shadow being led into his stable. As the handler closed the door, the dog in the shadows approached him, walking towards the light. "Well now, I must say these days they do seem to get more handsome."

Stepping into the light was none other than Velvet Sugar, a virtual icon in dog racing years past and holder of countless dog championships. She had even won championship ribbons in showmanship for her beauty. According to old tales from his mother, there weren't many who could match such raw talent in her day—beauty, speed, and composure.

Ramrod, almost speechless at the introduction, stammered, "I . . . I . . . I know you! My mother talked so much about you when I was a pup."

"That's right, sweetie, Velvet Sugar in the flesh."

"Wow. Did you know my mother? Liberian Queen? She said she knew you but failed to mention if you knew each other."

She shifted her weight now, trying to jog her memory. "Can't say that I do, sweetie. I've met many a dog in my time, you know."

Ramrod, persistent, continued. "You gotta remember her. She won a few crowns. Liberian Queen, she has this unmistakable white diamond shape on her forehead."

She now appeared to be thinking further back. "Oh yeah. Oh yeah, darling, now I remember a canine vaguely matching that description."

After a moment's pause, his excitement at her presence settled and he quizzically looked at her. "So what brings you here?"

Velvet Sugar looked at him in surprise, as if he didn't really know. "You mean you have no idea why I'm here this evening alone with you?"

"No, I don't. So you're going to tell me?"

She laughed. "How cute, my naive, strong racer. I'm here for you to make your contribution."

"My—contribution?"

"Yes, you handsome fool." She brushed against his body. "Your contribution to continue a winning bloodline."

Ramrod took two seconds' thought before catching on; it hit him like a pie in the face. "You're kidding me, right?" He began moving back as she continued to brush against his body. "I mean, you gotta be kidding me—you're old enough to be my mother."

Velvet Sugar, at first harshly drawing back from such a comment, now smiled. "Truthfully speaking, I'm old enough to be your grandmother, sugar pie." She continued her close courting. "Who knows, I might even be your grandmother."

"Wait a minute, wait a minute," he protested, pushing her away. "Is this the great 'Velvet Sugar' my mom told me stories about? How she single-handedly defeated all comers, capturing the Seven Crowns Pageant, and defied even human intervention as she swept through the transatlantic championships using a false name and won various dog shows without competitors coming even close to matching her radiant beauty?"

Velvet Sugar felt a moment of discomfort but shook it loose. "That's right, darling, it's all me in the flesh. Now, if you don't mind, let's us just hurry up and get this over, all right?"

"I'm stunned that a living hero, a female of your status, would let herself be degraded to this. How could you do this to yourself? How could you do this for a living? Have you no pride?"

Now feeling guilty she said, "Look, it's like you said—it's a living and I'm alive, ain't I? So, let's hurry up and get this over with. I'm not exactly too thrilled to be where I'm at today anyway."

"That's just it. Why do this if you're unhappy with your life,? Won't you in turn be more miserable, knowing full well that you are bringing more of yourself into such an unhappy life?"

She sighed. "Okay, so what are you talking about, whiz kid?"

"I'm saying, over the years, haven't you once wondered about the lives or conditions that your offspring must endure? I mean, it's a fact for the vast majority of them, life might have proven intolerable."

She stopped with a passing thought, then sat back. "You know something, baby, in all my seven years of life, I've had countless litters after my third year, and truthfully speaking, darling, I couldn't tell you where a single one of 'em's at, what their conditions are, or what they're doing . . . Over the years, darling, you tend to forget, and over time, you just don't care anymore. To me, it's just a living."

"I know you get tired of this. Don't you? When do you think it's time for it to all stop?"

"Don't you think I ever thought of that myself? After coming off the race circuit, my body was pumped with so many drugs for stamina, endurance, pain, vitamins—you name it. Hell, I was even taking drugs to counteract the drugs that I was taking. I'd never thought about any children no how. I was so far gone on all types of drugs—including fertility drugs—a litter didn't cross my mind. Sure, I was conscious, but I just didn't care. The many males that sired my litters have come and gone. Ha, I remember them pawing all over me as soon as I crossed the doorway." She laughed. "Never have I met one like you before. You're a first!" She began laughing hysterically.

"I don't want to 'contribute,' as you call it, for that cause. To me, it's simply a loser's cause."

She ceased laughing. "Lord, I don't believe this now. I must truly be old; for the first time someone has flat dusted refused my advances." She laughed again, as Ramrod added, "Entirely. I refuse to sire any offspring that shall in turn suffer the same fate as I."

She stopped laughing again. "Oh, and Your Gloriousness, how do you know that one pick of the litter that we might share won't be the answer to stop this madness that me and your mother and countless generations before have endured? How do you know?"

He sat in thought for a moment, then answered, "It's not likely."

She sat down in front of him staring him in the face. "You look, see I do what I do to survive. Look around you now. How many dogs do you know who, in two months, will be eight years old, huh? None of them—not a one. Now, look around again and tell me, how many dogs out there actually know their mothers or were raised by one? You see, both you and I are a rarity, don't you see, sweetie? And if I were you, I'd cherish that thought. Live life the way you're supposed to live it. Let the young take care of the young. They've been doing it. And if there's a change for the better, I say let's welcome it. Until then—"

She suddenly paused and looked as though she had finally found that light in the long dark tunnel she had been searching for so desperately. A tear left her eye as she moaned a whimpering howl of sorrow.

Ramrod stood up and approached her as she turned her back. "I'm so sorry if I've hurt you. Really."

"No, son, you didn't hurt me. You merely opened my eyes."

She lay at the opposite side of the bin. "All my life I've been running, running so fast, running so far away. Now I know what propelled me, made me run faster, always at my heels—it was the truth. All these years, I ran from it, feared it, avoided it, and tonight it caught up to me."

He tried to passively interject again, "Hey, I didn't mean to lay such a guilt trip on you."

"No, no, that's fine. You've just bared my subconscious thoughts I've had all along. So, if you please, I'll just leave you alone.

Ramrod stood looking at the living legend as she lay down before him on strands of straw, her only insulation from the damp, cold ground. As he stood over her in silence, he felt obligated to do something more for this former monarch of the dog kingdom.

"Can't you stop standing over me, staring, already? Why don't you fetch yourself over yonder side or something for the night? I won't bother to touch you."

He granted her wish, leaving her to herself.

The next evening, to Ramrod's surprise, Velvet Sugar returned. Her mood was chipper as she talked a little more, telling of her glamorous life and the customs she was fortunate to learn. She returned once more the following evening.

"You have a unique smartness about you, sugar plum, one I've never seen in all my years. While other dogs are being bred to run, seems like you were bred to think. I crossed a lot of mutts in my time, but never within our own breed have I known one to actually use his gray matter to think like you. You are truly a rarity."

After that night, she never returned. A week later, Ramrod found himself in cargo and traveling upon the circuit.

It had been three long weeks as the truck made its cross-country trek through the great states. They'd stopped off at various main cities and some rural counties for an occasional race. Some of the twenty-four dogs were left behind, others died in transit, and two were fortunate enough to be sold on the road at a truck stop for a hundred dollars each. Ramrod thought it lucky to have run across Winsome Winy at a broken-down track that had changed ownership as often as the weather changed in Kansas. Winsome was now a full-fledged mother raising a set of pups. She seemed happy when they briefly talked, yet there seemed to be a yearning inside of her that she felt hampered to disclose. He read it in her eyes but failed to make mention of it, in hopes that time would be a more bearable partner than the thoughts of what could've been.

Weeks later, he found that his group had whittled down to six dogs beating a path through such states as Colorado, New Mexico, Arizona, and California.

Later in the trip, he found out how conditions could get much worse, as the dogs stood for three months holed up in a seedy makeshift racetrack somewhere in Mexico. The track was actually a dirt road equipped with some type of gas power-built motor with an attached clothesline that dragged a white plastic bag at a high rate of speed across the dirt road. The locals and a few gringos, at times, came by to wager their money on the dogs.

The conditions there were awful, the food was scarce and distasteful, and only Ramrod and two of the other dogs remained alive from the original cargo. He was apprised of their situation the second day after they arrived at the track by an old greyhound named Greased Lighting, who was about twice the age of Velvet Sugar.

Greased Lightning suffered from paralysis of some type. He got around well with a two-wheeled cart permanently attached to his rear legs. He also wore a red bandana around his neck. "Whatever you do," he said, giving his first lecture to the incoming band, "don't venture further than five feet from the track during the course of the race or you're liable to be picked up by the locals. Remember, dog, in some of these parts, is still considered a delicacy. So, whatever you do, as soon as the race ends, hustle back toward camp. And by all means at night, stand close to the campsite in the light where it's safe! We lost quite a few dogs that way. Some even had the most harebrained idea, figuring to escape during the night or during the course of the race. If I failed to mention it, notice that we have no real gates to keep you trapped within. I guarantee you, those who attempted escape met with tragic failure. So, this here is your only safe outpost in a radius of three hundred or so miles. So, just do only what's expected of you to do, what you're born only for, and that's to run—and run fast."

After a month or so, the two who had remained from Ramrod's original group perished due to the harsh conditions of the terrain. Lovely One's body was still breathing when a track member sold him to a needy family.

"Betcha I know what's going to be the main course for Sunday dinner," one of the dogs proclaimed as they watched him depart.

Weeks passed and Ramrod was greeted with a welcomed surprise of sorts; he greeted, from an incoming convoy, his pal No Quarter. Also in the troop was Blue Jet, who seemed changed.

Ramrod gave his buddy No Quarter the lowdown on the camp. Of course No Quarter was terribly dismayed, but later, despite the rigorous conditions, he managed to adjust moderately.

The owners of the track later came up with a brilliant marketing scheme that would triple their attendance rates. Naturally, it involved two of their fastest dogs and altering the conventional dimensions of the track. It was billed as the greatest dog race in those parts ever. It had a two-week advertisement campaign, so the crowd already eagerly awaited what was billed "the race of death."

Unbeknownst to the participants, someone would fire upon them with guns to force them to run a mile straight away, then they were to jump across a twenty-five-foot or so ravine, where the first one across would be labeled the winner. The loser, if he didn't cross the ravine, would be shot. If he successfully jumped the ravine, his life would be determined by the attending crowd.

The undisputed two fastest dogs in the camp were Ramrod and Blue Jet. The two had a queer sense that the ongoing preparations and more than average allotments of food they had received were, beyond all doubt, some type of mystery brewing that involved them. The day before the grand event, the two shared their feelings of uneasiness and exchanged brief silent stares. The next day, the entire race grounds were packed with spectators.

As Blue Jet and Ramrod stood at the racing block feeling the searing midday heat overhead, the rest of the dogs stood fenced in with the best seats in the area. Spectators aligned the roadside as nearby armed men in a jeep revved the engine. As two handlers held the dogs, the plastic bag fluttered, escaping into the distance. The handlers released the dogs, who ran the pattern of the usual race until suddenly they realized that the jeep was following them. Then they heard the sound of bullets zinging behind them, which prompted them to run beyond their limit.

The crowd cheered as they witnessed the dogs reaching speeds as never before seen. The dogs, running neck and neck,

approached the ravine. Ramrod viewed a huge hole in his immediate path just before the ravine. Ramrod shouted to Blue Jet in
frantic fear to escape the hole, "Move over! I'm gonna trip over
a hole!"

Blue Jet, either not hearing due to the gunshots exploding
behind them or just plain concerned about saving his own
skin, didn't comply. Ramrod avoiding the hole just before the
ravine jump squeezed into Blue Jet's lane, knocking him off
balance. Ramrod successfully jumped over the ravine but
landed hard on his left front leg. Blue Jet, having to adjust during the course of his jump, fell short, falling into the fifty-yard
drop.

Ramrod turned to see the mishap caused indirectly to his
course redirection and looked upon Blue Jet's broken body
lying at the bottom of the ravine. Teenagers at the bottom of
the ravine fought over the spoils. Witnessing this, Ramrod had
an encompassing feeling that he just wanted to die. Dropping
to the ground, his front paw throbbed with pain as the crowd
cheered with satisfaction.

That evening the group huddled around Greased Lightening,
who paced back and forth while filling them all in on the track's
activities. "As you all might've guessed, the race was a success
and we've managed to gain publicity, good and bad. First, the bad
news: as usual, the World Animal Humane Society got tipped
off—always too little too late, if you ask me. Any hoot, they'll
make a 'surprise' visit to the camp come tomorrow. And the
good news is that among the many excited spectators was a
rich gringo who sought an interest in ole Ramrod there." Ramrod's attention focused. "Seems he's the proprietor of a Florida
Keys dog track, and he paid a hefty penny to acquire Ramrod.
So let's give a cheer to Ramrod, in the hope that maybe others
might be chosen down the line."

Ramrod remained silent and couldn't sleep throughout the
night. He relived seeing Blue Jet's broken body at the bottom of
the ravine over and over again. The following morning Ramrod

noticed the dogs had received double their food rations and had access to unlimited amounts of water.

"All right, you mutts, let's look lively. The WAHS agents will be here shortly. Why else do you think the bosses cut us some extra chow?"

After a little time passed, the dogs were alerted to a lone approaching jeep. When the jeep finally came to rest, out jumped a man and woman in similar dress, both wearing khaki and blue outfits with a patch on both arms that read WAHS. They both looked around the camp then greeted each dog, checking over their physical conditions. As the male agent surveyed him, Ramrod studied the arm patch closely.

"Hey there, boy. You're a nice-looking dog, considering." The agent looked over to his female counterpart. "If only they could speak, huh, Jean. Maybe this one could tell me a story."

Jean turned around to look at Ramrod. "In this hellhole, you can bet it would give me nightmares."

A few days passed. In his infinite wisdom, the co-manager of the track decided, against the wishes of the others, to cast a race featuring the winner of the famed "race of death" run. He planned to present it as a typical race, yet hoping that Ramrod's name would draw a more than average crowd. The others felt the potential for injury might jeopardize their already-negotiated sale of Ramrod; however, the race was still scheduled as a premiere race event.

Ramrod aligned alongside his long-time buddy, No Quarter and watched as the plastic bag quickly flew along the line. The handlers loosened their grips as the two dogs jetted off.

The dogs, racing neck and neck, were well focused and nearly halfway through the race when, out of nowhere, an unexpected distraction appeared that only Ramrod saw. Mystified by its presence, he turned off the track into the vast open field. His magnificent limbs stretched like smoothly flowing rubber. Just ahead of his front paws was the ever-elusive white rabbit. It had never been as close as now. Lengthening to a breakneck speed,

Ramrod found an elasticity he never knew existed within him, and he snapped at rapidly disappearing and reappearing rear paws as the rabbit kicked up dust and rocks that pelted Ramrod's mouth and eyes.

The white rabbit felt Ramrod's hot breath upon its feet and made a sudden ninety-degree turn to escape, temporarily throwing Ramrod off. He had only a microsecond of indecisiveness, but Ramrod's front left leg bent into an awkward, near-snapping position, shooting a hundred thousand volts of seething pain up his leg. But Ramrod was undaunted and overcome with his mad obsession. He gracefully rebounded and was within a salivating mouth's grip of capturing the rabbit. His mouth closed like a steel trap. He lifted his head; the race was over.

In that brief moment Ramrod reached a plane of existence that he'd thought never attainable in his life; his mouth closed around his most sought after trophy. Blood trickled from his tightened jaw. His overwhelmed senses blinded him to the pain in his leg as he walked with a limp. In his personal unseen utopia, he paced in a tiny circle lost in himself, ever turning inside the outstretched vastness of the open field. The three handlers who traveled the distance by jeep were unsure of how to handle such a never-before-seen sight. They sat in awe, watching the unusual ritual unfolding before them.

During the confusion that transpired, No Quarter went missing. He was never seen again. Ramrod, confident that No Quarter had escaped that night, dreamed that No Quarter successfully crossed the Mexican border back over to the States.

A week later, Ramrod found himself inside a kennel outside one of Florida's largest dog tracks. He stayed for a month and three days and ran in seven races. However, due to circumstances beyond his control or reasoning, he was carted off to a place near the Everglades in southern Florida called Dale's Puppy Farm. The front of the business was moderately presentable, and it had an enormous number of beautiful puppies.

However, two acres away from the main road, Dale's Puppy Farm owned a shack that was lost within the rural outback of the Floridian greenery. Surrounded by trees, shrubbery, snakes, and insects, the shack was a remote outpost and a far cry from any civilization. It also provided the confined setting for Ramrod and seventy other dogs.

The shack was without light, and the stench that crept beyond the four walls that bounded the isolated torture chamber led Ramrod to believe that he'd died and been sent to hell. This was Ramrod's sixth week here. He, along with the other residents, had lost a great deal of weight and took on the sad appearance of a skeleton rather than a live canine. Most of the dogs were so weak they couldn't bark, and they were fed a paltry portion once every three days. Every other week two men would arrive with masks on to remove the dead. One dog lay dead for five days in a cage shared by six others.

Ramrod was jammed inside of a three-dog-capacity cage with six other dogs where he and his cellmates stood in their own excrement. Two of the dogs were critically ill and lay underfoot. Ramrod's cage mates had been mentally beaten since their arrival to the farm. Many of them like Bobby, Jaggy, Thorton's Maiden, and Tube Steak had arrived as unwanted puppies that had matured. They knew they would die an agonizing death within a very short time, just like many of the others they'd witnessed over the months.

Bobby, Tube Steak, and Jaggy had, some time ago, plotted a daring escape. However, due to malnutrition they were too weak to escape—like the futile attempts of others past. Jaggy knew that Ramrod was the most recent arrival and a gifted athlete and figured he was the strongest and could attempt the escape better than anyone else.

The others nominated Ramrod for this duty, and he accepted with reservation since he didn't know who to run to for help. He thought that no one would care.

Tube Steak disagreed with him, giving him more insight into their scheme. "It's near this time. You see, once every three months or so, there's this woman who I remember used to come by when I was a puppy living on the farm."

"Yeah, it's true, I tell you!" Bobby shouted over the grumpy residents who were trying to discredit the story.

"Shut up, Bobby—I'm telling this, okay? So, anyways, she comes by to check over the place; checks inside the back rooms, the basement, and goes through it darn good. You see, the lady wears this patch on her arm."

"Heck, it scares those humans stiff," Bobby interjected.

"Hey," Ramrod said, silencing the room, "I know of that patch, and if I'm correct it has the same markings I encountered once in Mexico. It was supposed to be a group, a group of good people like you said, who are supposed to oversee our protection."

"That's a good one. I think the correct word is 'seen over.'" a dog grumbled his opinion.

"So what? Who cares? We gotta get help where we know we'll find it, and we need help now." A wolf mix named Timber Wolf rose to speak, bearing up his now-diminished, once-shaggy coat so that he resembled a lumbering stack of bones. "You sure it's around this time?"

Ramrod spoke. "I'll do it. It won't be easy, but I'll do it."

The three gave Ramrod an account of their plan. They surmised waiting around for the lady then trying to get her attention and leading her toward the path to the shack. "But she wouldn't hear us. Our voices are so weak that we can't bark," Bobby admitted.

"Well I can bark, that's no problem there. It's just that my legs are a little creaky—"

"You don't worry about that. I sez you'll do good." Tube Steak assured.

"You think so?"

"Yeah," Tube Steak said, nodding underneath him. "Tulip here ain't got much more to go on. Poor Bosco won't last another night."

Ramrod, now set at going, said, "All right, you three help me with this lock."

The creaky old lock took some doing, but they managed to unlock it through the broken cage fencing. Ramrod jumped down and, realizing his legs were like liquid, crashed and fell to the ground.

"You okay? You all right, fella?"

He stood up, steadying his balance. He now understood the real impact of being malnourished, his motor functions hampered as he swayed, trying to gather his balance.

"Take it real slow. Take it easy until you adjust," Jaggy said, slowing him up.

Giving himself a moment, Ramrod walked around the small shack. While he was adjusting, Timber Wolf offered his insight. "Before Dale left for his retirement home in the Keys two years ago, he kept me around as a mascot. I was an attraction for the kids. He bought me off this bankrupted wilderness resort park. It closed down ages ago. Anyway, Dale left the farm to two of his nephews, Mark and Wayne—"

"Murderers!" someone shouted.

"That they are! And dangerous. Don't let them get their hands on you, or you're finished! Anyway, those humans had a different idea about running the farm, more current to the 'out-of-date backward' business dealings their uncle had conducted over the years. Trimming this, cutting that, taking this, while they stuffed money into their pockets, only concerned with their own selfish needs. Soon after, when the county was low on money, the brothers wheeled and dealed and managed to convince the county to scrap the sharply increased funding of the county's dog pound and to let them handle the unwanted pets and strays—for a fee of course.

"Besides this one, I could tell you thousands of stories of abuse. I've watched it with my own eyes in shock. Anyway, an animal of my stature costs too much money to feed. Now, I knew what was in store for me, so I turned on them, chewed on Wayne pretty good too. He wanted to kill me then and there, but Mark's the smart one; he knew that during Dale's annual visit, if I wasn't around, he would question and search. So, they keep me here, barely alive, and six weeks prior to Dale's arrival, they fatten me up a bit. But this'll be the turning year for me, 'cause if this escape plan doesn't work, I will wait for Dale's visit. Soon as they release me to run out to greet him, I will immediately turn on them. And before they know what happened, I'll rip out both their throats."

Ramrod looked at Timber Wolf and knew at one time he had possessed the physical strength to carry out such a threat.

"This used to be a storage shack. Now it's a holding pen. It's part of Mark and Wayne's design to 'weaken and tenderize the meat to slow-baked'—what they call their exterminating methods."

Ramrod began feeling his normal leg strength and looked up to one of the windows, which had a divider that sectioned off the glass into four panes. One of the four panes had only a piece of cardboard covering a hole where the glass should have been. Climbing onto an old wooden barrel, Ramrod looked back. "I'm gone, people."

Listening to the many well wishes, he simply replied, "I'll do my best."

Pawing through the cardboard divider, he crawled out the opening. Recovering from this fall wasn't as bad as the first. His immediate sensation was the rush of clean, fresh air bombarding his nostrils. He had nearly forgotten how much he'd missed it and had actually taken it for granted. Walking a bit, he sniffed himself and realized he also missed the daily baths he'd received right up to the transition to Mexico.

"Well, enough of being concerned with myself and my own pampered life," he thought. "I've got to consider the others as well."

He walked through the bushes along the path, not wanting anyone to see him heading for the main road. As he walked through the foliage, he made an abrupt stop or two to gnaw upon edible vegetation. Coming upon the main road just inside the bushes, he looked across the street, and there sat the huge home that had been converted into Dale's Puppy Farm.

The front of the house contained a huge yard with a small three-foot fence circling the front right up to the main road, which connected to Highway 175 North. Ramrod figured the fence was to keep the twenty or so puppies that were scampering about the yard inside. Looking above at a big billboard advertisement, he saw an elderly man wearing a colorful hat with a bright smile, hoisting up a puppy alongside a little girl doing the same. The sign read: "Come and talk to Uncle Dale for a doggone good deal!" Underneath it, another bold-letter advertisement read: "Hurry! Come and see our exhibit! Timber Wolf—Mighty Canine of the Yukon!"

Ramrod sat around patiently all day scoffing up the passing insects that happened into his pathway and around. At night he wandered off for something to eat, but never too far. He luckily found a pool of water alongside the ditch where he sat for a cool drink. The next day, he stood dedicated at his post, his stomach still begging for food after the flimsy meal of beetles, one small lizard, an earthworm, and various leaves. He looked over across the street and watched two carloads of vacationing families as they petted the puppies. On the front porch, he witnessed Mark and Wayne, both holding puppies, greeting them with warm smiles.

Mark muttered to his brother, "I hope one of the cheap stiffs will at least pick out a ten-dollar puppy."

"I guess there's no hope in me holding this three-hundred dollar Dalmatian, huh?" Wayne asked.

"Nah, put him and the collie back in their cages. This bunch is small fish."

A teenager from the group walked up to Mark, inquiring about the billboard. "So, where's this exhibit of a Timber Wolf at?"

"Unfortunately, he's away sick for a week or so. Your father interested in buying a dog?"

Ramrod observed the business carefully. However, what immediately drew his full attention were the half-dozen or so puppy feeding troughs that were positioned across the yard. He watched as the puppies nibbled inside the huge bowls, for what seemed like forever, at a never-ending supply of food. As any hunger driven creature knows the mind isn't set for rational thinking. He sat there dreaming of how he deserved so much to eat his fill from those very troughs. As he watched, his hunger began to elicit feelings of anger in him at the pups for being so young and naive.

His mind then quickly jumped, and he began questioning the reason why he was sitting in some bushes starving. "I'm free now, ain't I? Let those dogs back in the shack fend for themselves. It wasn't my fault they got placed in such a predicament. Besides, Mom always told me I've gotta think of myself."

Ramrod, losing his grip on reality, was about to throw caution to the wind. He stood upon the threshold, about to charge across the road into the yard to eat from the troughs. Suddenly, something yanked him back; probably it was his logical mind resurfacing. He took a long, deep breath, and then patiently sat back to await the friendly woman with the specially designed arm patch. He waited for an agonizingly long two days.

In the ensuing days Ramrod was tortured watching the puppies eat heartedly from the troughs, and to add insult to injury, the final night, the area was covered with a torrential rain. Having no cover, Ramrod was soaked clear through to the bone and shivered in the cold night air.

This wasn't good for him, because his breed was accustomed to having little to no hair. He blessed the heat from the early morning sun. Rising up slowly to sit in its rays, he noticed he had gotten sick from the cold and now ached terribly. He passed out alongside the ditch until midday. He awakened, unnoticed by the passing motorists, with the sun beaming directly on top of him.

As he sat by trying to gather himself, Ramrod realized that the mental agony of hunger had a partner that was just as persuasive—illness. His logical, conscious reasoning had long since departed in the night while he was being drenched. He sat there, wickedly gaping at the enormous helpings of food. Ramrod was transformed into an enraged dog, possessed with quenching the pains of hunger. Across the street were four carloads of vacationing families who had stopped by the roadside so their restless kids could stretch their legs and pet the puppies. Mark and Wayne were busy inside the business—Wayne, catching up on paper work and Mark, cleaning cages.

Next door to the puppy farm sat an old, kindly neighbor who went by the name of Mildred. Throughout the years, she had set up her cold lemonade and sun tea stand, and earlier that day she had faithfully pitched her stand and sun umbrella. She was confident that with the day's steamy forecast, she'd turn over a nice profit. Besides, it was considered cathartic for her condition, as her doctors had been pushing her to get out more, get exercise, and mingle with people. She surmised she could get all of that running her stand—plus more entertainment than by watching the local TV provided by the stressed out parents trying to restrain their carsick children who ran amok.

Ramrod, not in his right mind and driven to satisfy his hunger, crept up the ditch onto the main road. Traffic was busy, yet it was currently clear. Mildred was the first person to see him. She shielded her eyes with her hands above her sunglasses to see better, thinking that she was looking upon a mirage. Ramrod, using his speed, cleared the main road in a quick second and descended down, then up, the ditch, hopped the three-foot fence, and then bowled over two puppies as he wildly commenced gulping down the contents of the nearest trough.

The children, watching in shock, began screaming and running to their parents. The situation caught Mildred's full attention, and she stood up. Ramrod finished the first bowl and ran over to the next one, knocking three puppies out of the way. A concerned parent screamed for the whereabouts of her child, while others drew shocking gasps from such a sight. "My God, look at him! He's totally emaciated," a lady with blond hair and sunglasses exclaimed.

"The poor thing's skin and bone. I've never seen such a horrible sight. Where did he come from?" another asked.

The lady with the blond hair and sunglasses picked up a full bowl of food and walked toward Ramrod. "Be careful, Mom!" her adolescent son cautioned her. Ramrod stopped eating to give an uneasy growl. She gently placed the bowl beside him as he wagged his tail in appreciation.

The customers' shrills finally caught Mark's undivided attention as he stood up, looking upon the perplexing situation. The lady with the blond hair coached her children, "Bring several more bowls to Mommy as quickly and quietly as you can, kids." As she took a closer look, she spoke to Mildred, "Miss, did you see which way this animal came from? This is a sad case of animal neglect. His owner should be reported to the proper authorities."

"He came from out of nowhere—just across that ditch in those bushes over there."

"I know greyhounds are slender," a man commented, "but I never seen one that bad before. You can see every bone in his entire body."

The next sight they witnessed was more shocking than the first as Wayne, charging the length of the yard, parted through the astonished crowd, encircled Ramrod—crazily swinging a stick—and crashed the stick twice upon the dog's back as he yelped. "Get outta here, you mangy mutt!" Wayne yelled.

The crowd was frozen in shock. Mark, who had earlier called out to his uncouth brother, trying to prevent what now unfolded before him, stood on the front porch, slapping his forehead and resting his hand over his eyes in disbelief over his brother's lack of tact.

After being hit, Ramrod darted through the crowd and crossed the ditch. He ran onto the busy road, just missing a car from one direction. Suddenly, a car coming from the opposite direction screeched its brakes, hitting Ramrod's rear hindquarters and sending him spinning into the ditch. The onlookers shrieked in agony. Weakened, he rose up limping and escaped, disappearing into the bushes.

Mildred jumped up, not saying a word, and she ran into her house.

"Mommy, that man hit the dog with that big stick," one of the children cried.

"Come on, children, we're leaving!" a mother yelled.

Mark made it off the porch and onto the grass, hoping he timed this just right to sway the popular consensus. "I know, folks, that was some sorry display, wasn't it?"

"You animal! The poor thing only wanted something to eat!" someone shouted.

"Yeah, I know, the poor thing's starved. He comes to our farm for handouts all the time. We fed him countless times. He belongs to some hick farmer just up a ways. Never feeds or cares for the poor bastaa—urr, ah, hum, I mean, poor dog."

"I don't care about that," an elderly man said, voicing concern. "The poor wretch was just hungry for a meal, and this baboon you hired here clobbered him. And you have the nerve to call this a puppy farm? And as for you, young man, had I been just twenty years younger, you'd be picking wood chips from your teeth now."

Ramrod sat in the path of the woods trying to calm down. He suddenly realized he was more mentally hurt than he was physically. "Of all the stupid things. I wish that darned car would've killed me. How could I do such a dumb thing?" He nervously looked back then limped into the bushes to hide. He had the time to be hard on himself, and he grilled himself even more. "Why did I have to be so selfish? Thinking only of myself, I just blew it for everybody. I traded them all in for four bowls of food. I failed, failed them all. I'm a failure. I let them down."

Wayne, at Mark's request, hurriedly closed up shop and shooed the customers away. Mark held a shovel, while Wayne had a sledgehammer, and they waited impatiently to cross the road, determined to straighten out their little mess once and for all.

Mildred looked out from her porch and covered her open mouth in horror.

Ramrod, hearing voices approaching ahead upon the path, ceased his self-pity to observe the two men walking down the path.

"We gotta destroy all lingering evidence now before they have some authorities or councilperson sniffing up our butts. We'd lose that county contract for sure and be out on the Florida strip washing cars for the rest of our lives," Mark counseled Wayne.

Ramrod quietly watched them walk to the end of the path, then to just beyond to the shack.

"Get in there, Wayne, while I finish digging this ditch and pull out three or four of 'em."

"But it smells bad in there."

"I told you, you bullheaded pig, to bring the masks, but like always, you refuse to listen—"

Ramrod, torn with confusion, raced for an answer. Off in the distance, he heard more movement in the bushes. His attention now twisted toward the yelping pleas of dogs calling for help, seemingly upon deaf ears. He dashed through the bushes to witness Wayne already executing Thorton's Maiden, Jaggy, and Tulip, whose lifeless bodies now lay upon the ground. He was about to exact a killing blow with his sledgehammer on the downed Timber Wolf.

"I saved the best for last. I've been waiting for this moment for a long time, you flea-infested heap!" he said, crashing the hammer down with all his might.

Ramrod jumped in shock.

"Quit stalling, that's enough," Mark called to Wayne. "Now get in there and get out the rest of that smelly vermin, so I can hurry up and cover them before I puke."

Mark looked over and saw the bushes move next to Wayne. He then watched Wayne drop the hammer and mysteriously shriek in pain as he turned around and reached behind himself for something seemingly invisible. Wayne unsuccessfully attempted to shake loose the greyhound whose teeth were now latched onto the rear upper-right part of his thigh.

Mark, at first totally shocked, swung the shovel, crashing it across Ramrod's head. Ramrod let go, but Mark struck him with another crushing blow. Ramrod aimlessly wandered, muddled and dazed, back through the bushes onto the path.

Wayne cried in pain.

"Quit crying, stupid. Had you been more careful, you woulda seen 'im coming. Now go over to the path over there. I thought I seen him fall, so you can finish him off now!"

Wayne, armed with his ten-pound sledgehammer, searched through the bushes to extract his vengeance.

Meanwhile, at the foot of the woods near the road, the blond-haired woman and a conservation officer had already searched the approximate area and were working their way up a path they stumbled upon, she hoped it would lead to the malnourished, car-struck dog she'd encountered earlier at the puppy farm.

Wayne found and cornered Ramrod, who was too disoriented to flee. Ramrod knew that he had no recourse for salvation and accepted his fate with pitiful eyes as he looked upon his executioner. He cringed and drew his last breath, hoping his final sensation before death—pain—was brief, yet he closed his eyes in anticipation of ultimate pain. The first stroke of the heavy steel hammer collapsed bone and soft tissue, and Wayne returned it hastily to produce another full arc swing.

The blond-haired lady and the conservation officer finally found Ramrod, but they weren't prepared for the ghastly sight before them. They watched helplessly as Wayne brutally struck the dog many times over in a swearing fit, while his lifeless body reverberated from the blows.

"Stop it right there!" the officer demanded.

Mark, hearing the commotion, ran over to see what was going on, absent-mindedly holding the bloody shovel in full view. Shattered, the blond-haired lady crouched down in tears to hold onto Ramrod's still paw. The paw was permanently fixed, extending outward in a gesture that she interpreted as a plea for mercy.

The conservation officer, overwhelmed at such a sight, dispatched a crew to collect evidence and take pictures. As customary, the officer detained Wayne and Mark for an hour of questioning and then released them pending a court date.

Over the months, try as she might, the blond-haired lady couldn't forget the haunting touch of Ramrod's reaching, lifeless paw—it had a profound impact upon her. Unable to blot out such a terrible recording in her mind of the neglected dog she'd befriended, she requested his name from the conservation officer. In tribute to him and other animals suffering the same fate, she spearheaded a grassroots rally. Armed with such incendiary evidence as the Dale's Puppy Farm incident and others she gained through research, she generated a barnstorming campaign that netted the specific concerns of domestic animal and animal humane lobbying groups wilderness and wildlife lobbying groups.

Further down the road and after years in the making through their combined efforts, these groups became the pioneers who laid the groundwork that assisted lawmakers in passing legislation to formulate the Animal Rights Act, a law that documented guidelines and restrictive care for animals within man's care. This law was aptly named the Ramrod Act. The Ramrod Act brought closer scrutiny to the plight of mistreated animals at shelters, pet shops, and other facilities across the United States

* * *

Brian felt his heart sinking and, sympathizing with Ramrod, said, "My Lord, he'd lost his mother, and instead of being gutted with hatred and indifference, he found it within himself to pull together. Such inner strength that I know many lack in today's world."

"True, my insightful aide, his altruistic sacrifice is noted, and in his name shall flourish protection for his kind. Yet there are others who share his gift, who I'm sad to say, sacrifice mainly for man's greater good—"

11736

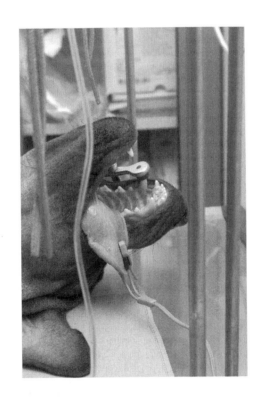

Strange as it may seem, this stately structure, with its steril-
ized apparatuses, elaborate machinery, perpetually waxed
floors, and infinitely sanitized white rooms, is home sweet
home.

"Eleven, seven, thirty-six? One, one, seven, three, six! Doctor,
he seems to not be coming around this time."

Another voice spoke. "Mark those readings!"

"Blood pressure falling low! Eleven thousand, seven hundred,
thirty-six, do you hear me?"

"Heart rate is bottoming out, Doctor. He's going to flatline
on us!"

"Don't do this yet, one, one, seven, three-six. Hang in there,
baby. We still need you! Nurse, stand by with that resuscitator!"

There they go again [*sigh*]. You know, it's a mystery to me
why these people get so worked up over a washed-up has-been
like me. The name's 11736. Don't ask me why. To the best of
my thinking ability, I'd figured it as a lab number. I'm nothing
important, only known by merely another number this lab gives
to all of its research animals. I came to this research facility
here in Ann Arbor, Michigan, nearly a year—no, two years ago.
Hmm, or maybe six months ago? Heck, I don't know. I don't
even remember my real name, it's been so long. It seems like
ages.

There's not much I recall these days. I go under anesthesia
quite often now—more than usual—however, I do know that
I'm a Siberian husky! Well, you wouldn't know it by my appearance, 'cause they shaved off most of my hair to monitor the skin
lesions on me. It all would have eventually fallen out anyway.

Oh, and I do know I pulled competitively in a dog team in
the famous annual Triad dogsled race in Alaska once. My group
didn't win, but I had the satisfaction of participating. I remember
the frozen, arctic cold of the great Alaskan Far North. I loved
the cold. The camaraderie among your sled team, along with the
free and open country experience of the frigid North, was a
sheer conquest into the unknown. It's sort of funny, but I kinda

get that feeling now. Every time I go under, it feels like I'm the lead team dog trudging into the unknown!

I remember a few friends at this lab, like Numbers 3731, 271, 902, 18511, 16660, and 18301.

Number 3731 is a Rhesus Monkey. He has antennas. They implanted these weird electrodes into the base of his brain—some type of scientific study in the area of "human" behavior. Hey, it's a mystery to me. The gang teases and laughs at 3731, telling him that we are still waiting patiently for HBO reception. At times it's the only way to keep what sanity you have left. If 3731 were able to understand, he would laugh. He appeared to have great communication skills when he first arrived.

Number 271 was a feline. He died of an electrical shock—that far surpassed the specified upper-margin levels—at the hands of some inexperienced, last-minute, substitute graduate assistant.

Number 902 is much livelier. He's a raccoon used in reaction-sequences lab work. I like 902. He likes to joke and kid around, and he rattles my cage now and then in friendly gesture.

Numbers 18511, 16660, and 18301 are all canine newcomers that are protectively pampered by WAHS, an animal rights activist group. Numbers 16660 and 18301 are used in radiation experiments in the study of long-term and specialized radiation effects, and Number 18511 came from a space-experimentation facility where they tested the effects of weightlessness on internal body organs. They were lucky enough to be subject to the new guidelines in the Animal Rights Act that was passed just two years ago. But I don't qualify. I have been on the experimentation circuit for a while; being a part of various experiments in five previous labs, I've been passed down in the system.

No, this was definitely not like the days of old.

I was sought after principally because of my strong, pumping heart. After several research labs in pharmaceutical chemistry finished with me, they booted me over to cancer tissue study and malignant liver cancer tumor care. Yes, I believe these new guys are too pampered. Look at me. In the old days, before the advent of animal rights legislation, it wasn't uncommon for all dogs like me to have their vocal cords cut to reduce the level of noise in the environment. Also, being neutered was a definite must. It kept down the number of fights and made us more "tame." I was singled out, chosen by luck of the draw at one of the previous labs to be the focus of a study on the chronic effects of specialized cancer patients who were bedridden. For that study, the doctors severed my spinal cord. But believe me, I'm not bitter. Really! They've since treated me real good—this lab being the standout best, though. They somehow knew I was a Siberian husky, even though all my hair had fallen out from those lesions. That, in my mind, was truly amazing.

One of the lab assistants here takes me out from time to time. She carries me on a stretcher and even places me in the snow! Somehow, she knows I love this. Being in that deep snow at night in the subfreezing chill of a Michigan winter, closing my eyes under that beautiful full moon, just takes me back. Me, who once was a remarkable work dog ... who proudly participated on a sled team ..." [11736 gets choked up at this thought.]

"Doctor! Doctor! We're losing him again! Eleven seven thirty six, do you hear me? Don't quit on us yet! Oh no!"

"Okay, continue CPR compressions, increase his injection dosage, then stand clear for another double prong sizzle."

Yeah ... yeah this lab treats me better than all the rest. I remember that last research facility. What a bunch of sadist they were! They were so unconcerned with the lives of their test animals—Me for example. Instead of stitching me up after various operations, too numerous to count—and allowing me to heal properly, they would instead staple my incisions together, and treat me with some chemical agent to prevent the natural healing process so they could readily access my internal organs, which could be poked and pried at will. Talk about your sense of feeling violated! In all truthfulness, I felt as convenient as an open-and-close lunchbox.

I know my being experimented on is for the betterment of animals and humans alike, to fight against rare and common diseases, but it pains me when they forget that I, like them, am a living being. But being here, in a four-star establishment, I'm treated like I should've been treated—like anyone who's under the spotlight. I'm one of their star performers. Yeah, that's what I am! One who braves the unknown. Me, 1173 . . . 6. Yeah . . . if . . . I . . . I cl . . . close my eyes . . . I . . . can still . . . feel the . . . arrr . . . tic win . . ."

"11736! Doctor, Doctor!"

"I . . . fe . . . e . . ."

"Okay, everyone—on three! Clear!"

"Fe . . . thhhuh . . . a . . ."

"No response!"

". . . I . . ."

"Come on, eleven seven thirty-six, please pull out of it! All right, everyone, stand ready for another try!"

". . . ———— . . . ———— . . ."

"Doctor, should I increase his injections?"

"———————— . . . ————————"

"11736? On three, for another go 'round. Stand clear, here we go! Please, oh please, this time!"

". . . ————————"

"That's it, Doctor, he flatlined."

"Okay [*sighs*]. Did we get it all on record? Tag him and send him for an autopsy. Nurse, do we have an approximate time of—"

* * *

Brian stood, astonished.

"True, my Angel Brian, some creatures honestly contribute to the betterment of all. And then we have those like our next hero, the ones not a soul would expect to donate their lives to save a valued few."

Brian, uncertain whether to question or make statement, said, "Those souls are special in their own right, Lord."

"Yes, my coveted angel, those souls have a special place within all our hearts, and I'm inclined to think you believe likewise—"

Robbie

The city lights flickered and wavered dimly. It was 1983, two hours past the witching hour. In the still of the night, in a Lower East Side business, two men knelt surreptitiously. One closely held a red-bulbed flashlight, hoping the illumination wouldn't give them away.

"Darn it, Smooth, I still can't see a thing with that blasted red light. This was your idea anyway!"

"Here," Smooth held the flashlight's beam closer to the safe's lock while his companion, Rippy, affixed a drill to the lock. "And this is the thanks I get for attempting to reduce the chances of us being seen—an assistant's work is never appreciated, I tell you."

Rippy triggered the drill, and the high-pitched, piercing whirl of the motor meshed with his voice. "That mutt of yours out there is awfully quiet. I hope he's at his post and not somewhere goofing off, or I'll tell you!"

"Rippy! Such lack of faith by you is definitely not becoming. You know as well as I—no news is good news with Robbie. My compadre shall warn us if need be. We've grown together, him and me. We trust each other. He wouldn't let me down, never in a million years. I still say you should reconsider our—"

"Enough of that already, will you? I've got enough on my mind, so can the talking about that trash!"

Smooth, whose real name was Aaron Davis, momentarily fell silent, affixing the light into its needed position. "How much— ten minutes out. How much farther down the road are we?"

"Two minutes, this lock will be popped, and in five, we ought to blow out of here—hope that dog's got his ears on, given that this is possibly a silent alarm. We'd have ten minutes tops before those 911 operators make the call to the police—"

"With my estimations, in twenty to twenty-five minutes the police should be rolling up, so with Robbie as watchdog, we've got an extra five minutes. Also, I might add, given the five bogus calls my cousins phoned in at various ends of the precinct as insurance approximately ten minutes ago, we've got fifteen minutes tops."

"So, you think you got this well planned?" Rippy grunted as he pried the damaged lock off and the door swung open.

"Sure. Right down to a science. And, if we don't play it too sloppy, we'll always be five minutes ahead of our Motown city police."

Rippy laughed as he began stacking money and blank checks into a sack.

"A science huh? Well here, scientist, help me stack the rest of this money so we can blow this place."

With their job complete, the two burglars snaked through the winding interiors of the building, making way for their exit. With the confines of the dwelling near pitch black, the two, professionals at their trade, used only the lights from the Exit signs, a random security light, and the exterior lighting that was beaming in to guide them.

Rippy came to a sudden dead stop, and Smooth's momentum carried him forward, crashing into Rippy's back.

"Wait a minute—lookie here. It's an ICAN Series 9000 Double EX computer."

"Oh yeah. Well, that's something I'll keep under my hat so the next time I see one, I can honestly say I can identify it. Now, let's move. We've got less than a minute!"

"No, no Mista Smooth Aaron, you don't understand. This here computer sitting before us is top of the line machinery, and I mean top of the line. Do you know what the going rate for one of these babies is? There isn't another computer made that can top it."

Smooth, growing impatient said, "Come on, Rip baby, we ain't got time for this here. We gotta move!"

Rippy made a sarcastic snicker and replied, "For an ICAN Series 9000 Double EX—I'll make time."

Smooth, holding onto the loot bag, felt edgy and uneasy. He looked frantically out various windows as Rippy began stripping the wiring from the wall and winding it around the computer console. Rippy grunted as he lifted the entire system and lumbered off behind Smooth. Walking down the remaining hall near the open window they had used as an entrance, they both froze in their tracks as they heard Robbie's signaled barking.

"See, I told you, idiot!" Smooth said, scolding Rippy as he dropped the computer console right where he stood. Seeing headlight beams flash close by, they both darted down just below the window, taking deep breaths.

"Think they seen us?"

"No, my greed-warped partner in crime. If procedure dictates, they'll check the front closely first, which'll buy us possibly enough time to get out of here by the skin of our necks if we only take the loot!"

"Yeah, yeah. Sure. Sure, of course."

Smooth, peeping out the window, watched closely as the police car's taillight turned the corner. "Let's go!" Smooth tossed the loot out first then followed. As he stood up, he said in a hurried whisper, "Come on, come on. They'll be around that corner in a matter of seconds!"

Rippy jumped through, and both men ran away from the well-lit rear of the building towards the security provided by the dark alley.

Robbie, hiding amidst the bushes near the business, waited on cue for both officers to abandon their marked unit and investigate the building. He let out a deep sigh of relief after hearing the familiar fleeing footsteps escape. He'd always hated putting plan B into practice, since this diversion tactic was quite risky with the police. On two separate excursions, he had come close to being shot when he attempted to distract them away from his long-time, inseparable best friend, Smooth. But for Smooth's safety, he would consider swimming the Amazon River filled with starving piranhas. They both had indeed come a long way.

From a safe distance between two garages, Smooth reached out his arm to stop Rippy, who was ahead of him. Panting hard Smooth said, "Stop! Stop! Wait!"

"Oh no! Not this again," said Rippy. He winced, trying to catch his breath.

Smooth got a big kick out of watching Robbie creep alongside the opened police car door, raising his leg toward the front seats. Smooth bowled over with laughter.

"Come on. Let's make it back to the spot so we can divvy this up!"

Smooth watched his pal make a safe departure and turned to leave at Rippy's request. Twenty minutes later they stood inside the "spot," which was nothing more than the basement of an abandoned home where Smooth, with his many talents, had rigged a working light overhead.

The room was sparsely furnished with an old wooden table with multiple layers of paint showing through its peeling finish and two broken chairs supported by old books.

Rippy was elated as he counted their loot. He focused mainly on the endless stream of bills passing through his hands.

"So, you still won't honor my buddy's share in the business?"

Rippy, half listening said, "No. We'll discuss it—two thousand fifty, two thousand one hundred fifty—later. Look! Look at this. You made me mess up the count!" Rippy raised his hands in an upset gesture.

Smooth's eyes followed Rippy's discomforting gesture and observed a gun handle slightly concealed under Rippy's belt.

"Hey, what is this stunt you're trying to pull? I told you I don't work with guns! I thought I made that perfectly clear."

"What? This thing here?" Rippy asked, pulling out the nickel-plated .25 caliber automatic pistol and trying to sound innocent. "This here is our security blanket."

"What are you talking about, Rippy? I've made it simple enough from the beginning for even you to understand. No guns, and above all, *no* shooting at any cops or security guards. They're just doing their jobs."

"No, no, no, my partner, it isn't about that. You forget so quickly what my old profession was." Smooth's expression changed as he looked at Rippy. "Remember, I still have people after me, and besides, we need protection carrying our loot from a break-in back to the 'spot,'" Rippy reminded Smooth.

Smooth stood in Rippy's face, unwavering in his stance. "Sorry, Rip, but I ain't buying neither one of those stories. 'Sides, if we're on our way back from a break-in job and we just happened to get mugged, I'd say that's justice's way of slipping us with a pie in the face and leave it at that. But I don't work around any guns. I guess that means you'll have to find yourself a new partner."

With that declaration, and without hesitation, Smooth did an immediate about-face and headed toward the exit.

Rippy, detecting the seriousness of Smooth's voice, called out and, observing the possible finality of the situation as Smooth turned away to leave without his cut, said, "Wait, wait, wait. Hold up there, Aaron. Look, if you say no guns then there's no guns. Now, why don't you hold out your hand for a share of this loot?" Rippy began to laugh. "Better make that two hands."

Like clockwork, Robbie, appearing out of nowhere, sounded winded as he panted alongside Aaron's legs. Rippy glanced down at him, gave a tired sigh, then up, while he counted Aaron's share. Rippy beat Aaron to the punch. "Don't even ask!"

Thirty minutes or so later, into the early morning, Aaron and Robbie walked through the city streets listening to the chirps of the waking birds before both departed for home.

Aaron looked down apologetically at Robbie. "Listen, Robbie boy, you did an excellent job tonight, and don't worry, I'm still at bat for you against that stubborn Rippy not wanting to cut you in the gang for your fair share and all. You take risks just like the both of us."

Robbie, a scrappy-looking, smorgasbord mixture of retriever, spaniel, German shepherd, and Irish wolfhound, gave him a look of solemn, tired affirmation while his tongue flopped haphazardly as he walked. The variety of breeds within this one dog would immediately gain him the label of mutt, but with his expressive eyes and sixth sense in interpreting humans, one would think him not far removed from human. He stood at a medium height—from a dog's perspective—with wooly black and gray fur, with patches of white sprinkled here and there. His uncommon gait appeared lopsided and top heavy, and as he walked, he looked as if the majority of his weight was shifted onto his front paws. Aaron, stopping in the middle of the street under a streetlight, looked at the time.

"Hey sport, you better head home to your family. It'll be daybreak soon."

Robbie, now picking up his pace, departed in the opposite direction. Aaron stood, watching him run off.

"Hey, I'll see you soon, right? Don't run off and get yourself killed now!"

Aaron watched Robbie gallop until his silhouette disappeared into the pre-dawn darkness. Aaron walked home with his take securely tied to his chest beneath his coat. Now able to breathe easy after the job, he walked the length of his journey, dreading the next one. That was if he chose to accept another job. Aaron usually didn't have much say about the choice of jobs in his partnership with Rippy, but he did, however, have the power to voice his objections. If he judged—for any reason—not to go, they both didn't. They were always successful, except the one time Robbie didn't show and they were both captured inside a building by the police and booked.

Yeah, that Robbie has always been good luck, every since he wandered into my life, Aaron thought. *Wandered into my life . . .* he drifted back.

At the age of nineteen, Aaron had two years of college, majoring in electrical engineering. However, due to a nervous breakdown, he eventually dropped out. Months passed, and with the aid of an aunt who worked at one of the major car factories, he managed to gain employment at the Chrysler Dodge Main Plant. There, he worked with dedicated service for fourteen years on the assembly lines with hundreds of other fine workers until it closed its doors permanently. There were a lot of excuses with big words, such as stagflation, robotics, price-cutting for competitive measures, the Japanese product, government cutbacks, the trickle-down effect, etc., but for him, those words were just a smoke screen. The harsh reality of his situation struck unmercifully when his unemployment compensation depleted to zero. He lost his home, his dignity, and everything in life for which he had worked so hard.

Aaron's experience with welfare was a bitter lesson in futility. He was submerged in a maze of unending paperwork that had led him on wild goose chases, unexpected dead ends, pitfalls, loopholes, and never-ending prerequisites, supplemental and ghost paperwork. Also, the social workers he dealt with weren't the most compassionate or sympathetic. Here he was at the end of his rope, his whole life flushed down the toilet, and the three social workers who were servicing him broke off in an argument over which fried chicken restaurant they'd prefer for lunch that day. It wasn't too surprising that after enduring such an ordeal he suffered another breakdown. He was reduced to living on the streets and carrying all his worldly possessions in a metal pushcart. If he could remember correctly, it was three months later that Robbie had wandered into his life. They both lived and shared the hobo life together. As time passed by, Robbie was always by his side—his protector, so to speak.

Aaron eventually shored up a great deal of strength and overcame the trauma of his breakdown. He was quick to give credit to Robbie and his companionship in prompting his recovery. It was during this time that Aaron was convinced that he and Robbie were mysteriously connected telepathically. After his recovery, Aaron wouldn't see Robbie for a few weeks at a time, then one day he would have a vague thought of Robbie in the back of his mind, and out of the blue, he would pop up.

Robbie had learned through his vagabond lifestyle that he had many families and self-proclaimed owners. Once he had counted eight different owners! He didn't mind really, but at first, it proved somewhat of a shock. Now he had an understanding and thoroughly accepted their relationships even more, for rather than being his master—or so-called master as the others had titled themselves—he recognized Aaron or "Smooth" simply as his buddy. And on that level, the relationship they shared was free and equal, a bond unlike the others. Except there was one other relationship that Robbie shared that put his relationship with Aaron second in priority and which Robbie knew might make Aaron feel a bit slighted, but he also knew in all practical sense that Aaron shouldn't mind. Robbie was quickly heading toward that owner's house right now, his first and true owner: a special little boy named Devon.

Robbie slipped through the basement window of the apartment, which was always open, and steadily climbed two flights of stairs, holding his position in the hallway momentarily to listen for any sounds from the apartment two doors down. His eyes displayed a look of uncertainty and worry, for Old-Man Honeycutt resided in the apartment and had it in for him. Old-Man Honeycutt had a strange and passionate hatred for all four-legged types. Armed with his butcher knife, the old man had chased Robbie many times through the apartment dwelling.

Robbie scratched carefully on his owner's door, awaiting an answer and keeping a sharp eye on Mr. Honeycutt's door. After a few moments of anxiously scratching and waiting, the door swung wide open as if he was expected. He gently took two steps through the doorway then paused.

"Well, this is definitely a first for you. You're back early from a night of hanging with the fellas!" Audrey Campbell sarcastically snapped, speaking down to him.

Miss Audrey Campbell was Devon's mother. To this day, Robbie could never fully understand why she had carried an attitude towards him. She was dressed in an oversized robe, house shoes, and curlers that had hair strands sticking out in an awkward array that would've awakened the dead.

As his guilt-ridden eyes slowly looked up, scanning the length of her seemingly towering body—his way of exchanging an uncertain "Hi"—he met her eyes quickly then dashed off towards Devon's room. He strangely always expected a swift kick to his rear as he ran by, but then he guessed it was substituted with the usual barrage of lip bashing he got. He slowly crept into the room as two tiny eyes opened, following his gait until he rested alongside the bed.

"And I wish I could live in someone's home, stay out all night, be provided with food and shelter, and not be expected to do a doggone thing," Audrey continued. "But Devon wants a dog—you, not a *real* dog. What in the world he wants your tramp butt for, I'll never know, and—"

Robbie let out an exaggerated long sigh, his eyes looking as if to say, "Well, she's at it again." Audrey had changed into her clothes, and while standing in front of the mirror putting on her makeup, she continued her ongoing verbal assault.

Robbie looked around the room to observe nothing unusual. *Might as well check to make sure everything's okay*, he thought.

The flashing instrumentation on the machines and the muted beeps and chirps signaled no signs of trouble. The numerical LED readout seemed to be at its constant rate. Devon's full IV bag flowed in its usual timed, continuous fashion. Robbie took a breath, then spoke to himself, "Yep everything checks out. Now all I have to do is wait for her tirade to end, then I can finally get some rest."

Audrey's rambling flowed onward as Robbie watched her kiss Devon then put on her coat. Finally she yelled out, "And don't let me catch you laying your dirty, smelly hide on his bed!"

Well, that's the period, Robbie thought while taking a tension-clearing breath. He then hopped onto the foot of the bed as he heard the door slam. Feeling a small gentle hand's feeble attempts at brushing the back of his coat, he crawled closer to give easier access. After five half strokes, it collapsed out of weakness, not being able to rub anymore.

"You . . . you came."

"Didn't think that I'd make it, huh?" Robbie asked, looking over to Devon.

"I'm glad you did."

They both closed their eyes, resting, as the kidney dialysis machine and IV pumped their fluids, the heart and blood pressure monitors also fused onto his body. A huge oxygen tank and mask stood within Devon's reach. A phone connection was close by with an emergency medical button for ambulance, police, and fire, if needed. Also labeled on the connection was Audrey's number at work and the number for the attendant care nurse who was due to check in on him in a matter of hours. Nothing changed; the machines in the room continued their usual pattern as both boy and dog lay in peaceful slumber.

Aaron, in turn, finally made it home to his small, and claustrophobic one-bedroom apartment. He looked around at the peeling, paint-chipped walls and the floor with a half-dollar-sized hole that looked down into his neighbor's apartment—which he had covered with a throw rug from the local resale shop. He walked over and picked up an object to bang on the radiator that leaked rusty brown water onto the floor, while the cockroaches humored themselves by playing a suicidal game of dare, scattering underneath his footsteps. His next-door neighbor was drunk again and playing his old scratched Sonny Stitt and Wes Montgomery albums at full volume while battering his mate. Aaron shook his head, smiled, and thought to himself, "Yeah, 'be it ever so humble,' as the song goes, 'there's no place like home.'"

Taking his money belt off, he placed half the money into a specially designed compartment in the back of his dresser drawer. The other half he stashed within the confines of the ceiling tile. "No sense in keeping all yo' eggs in one basket," he said, mocking his great-grandfather from Louisiana. Aaron wondered what his great-grandfather—if he were still alive—would think of his great-grandson, the thief.

Aaron thought back to the beginning of his work in his illegal occupation; it was nothing short of a baptism by fire. The opportunity presented itself just shortly after he met up with Robbie. The opportunity, of course, being Rippy. Not too long before meeting Rippy, Aaron had reached the gutter-level of human ambition and was more than ready to "cash in the chips."

Rippy credited himself for being the one to pull Smooth off the streets through his own skillful and shady market dealings. Aaron's initial job was to simply "hold" a stash for him, or run the stash from point A to point B.

Yet Aaron, with all his hardships, still had ethics, and his resolve was clear on drugs; he despised them and considered their use to be slow suicide. Speaking from personal experience, he described his few hits as a temporary joyride that, when gone, left him to inevitably crash-land into his darkest fears in hell—alone.

Nevertheless, in his community where jobs were nil, morale was low, and constant despair and hopelessness about an unforeseen future reigned supreme, drugs flourished. Drug use ran rampant and drugs were as accessible as your average McDonald's hamburger. But more than all of his previous reasons put together, he hated drugs because he had witnessed the very young being seduced and consumed by this fire.

Rippy admired Aaron for being strong-willed in his stance to have him cease peddling drugs and found it surprising to see how someone who was at the bottom of the barrel could still possess such pride. It was soon after that Rippy, feeling his age, knew drug dealing was an occupation he'd prefer leaving to his competitive younger peers. Besides, he cared to live longer.

That's when Aaron, feeling guilty and seeing how this drug cancer had eroded the community at large, was about to jump ship, but then he decided to stay on when Rippy chose to set up his own little ring and go into the breaking and entering business. Aaron figured his risk factor was cut in half. He didn't have to worry about the unpredictability of greed-mongering drug dealers or hot, young, armed, rival upstarts with a hairpin trigger. His only concerns were the police, maybe a security guard, security camera, or burglar alarm. No problem.

Besides, as Rippy said, "It's practically a racket. A business has items that the owners have quoted at ridiculous prices. They wait for us, like a Santa Claus in the night, to come rip them off of a few things. They log it onto their insurance claims at nearly twice the cost, along with other more expensive items they list as stolen but are actually packed and boxed somewhere in the basement. Also, they exaggerate the damages done so the insurance'll kick in an extra thousand or two. They make a buck. The insurance company will do their year-end tabulating, come up with some numbers, and due to the increased number of B and E's in that sector, they jack up their premiums. They make a buck. Then the community needs police, security guards, and equipment. Those guys make a buck, and in turn we make a buck too. So, the money constantly changes hands, and in anybody's schoolbook that's considered a business. I can live with that—it's the American way."

Aaron naturally had a different opinion. Still, he figured if stockbrokers' lawyers could swindle the government and businesses out of millions of dollars and only receive a slap on the wrist or a short time in a posh federal pen and if mass murderers who were actively sought by writers and directors could make millions for book and movie rights to their graphic reenactments—then he had a right to profit too. And considering the government, which spent billions on stimulating overseas economies when it couldn't care for its own cities—while claiming the nation is in a trillion dollar deficit—and the fact that half of the factories in America were now permanently shut down and the other half worked a skeleton crew and weren't hiring, Aaron figured the country was going to hell in a hand basket anyway, so he might as well ride the crest of the wave until it all came crashing down.

He stretched himself out on his lopsided mattress and took a tired breath as the morning sunlight peeped through the shades, poking at his itchy eyes. Thinking of the huge sum of money they had netted, it wasn't long until he was snoring in a sound sleep.

* * *

Several blocks from her residence, Audrey Campbell hurriedly walked the distance to her place of work, Big Motor City Market, hoping to punch the clock on time and not be docked again like she was on Friday. She hoped increasing her speed would serve two purposes: first, she might actually arrive to work early and second, the movement would possibly increase her blood flow enough to raise the temperature in her cold body on this late February morn.

Hearing footsteps from behind would normally cause her great concern, however these fast-approaching footsteps sounded like those of a woman. Audrey, not looking around, figured the other woman was probably also running late, but then Audrey felt a light touch on her left shoulder. Immediately her city survival skills honed in as she balled up her fist and hoped that after striking with the first blow, she would have enough time to reach into her purse for her knife.

"Missus Campbell, Miss Campbell? It's me. Sorry if I startled you."

The familiar voice registered, and Audrey exhaled a full, tension-clearing sigh and turned to face Dr. Val Larson, who was adorned in a beautifully colored African ensemble with a lavishly designed matching headpiece, from which flowed a lengthy tapestry of cornrows. Had Audrey not been angered not only by Dr. Larson startling her but also by her mere presence, she would've asked her out of "fashion curiosity" to open her coat for a brief peek at her ensemble's wonderful design.

"Miss Campbell, I hope you will reconsider my proposal. Please, I strongly believe this could benefit the health of your son, Devon."

"No, Dr. Larsons. A thousand times no. I've told you already. Now would you just get out of my face? I'm late for work!"

Dr. Larsons was persistent and continued, "But, Miss Campbell, you're not looking at this serious issue in the proper perspective—"

"Proper? Proper? Sister, you've got a lot of nerve saying 'proper.' Now get out of my face or else I'll report you for stalking—it's a new Michigan law. Of course, you know that by now, Dr. Larsons. If you really are a doctor. From what I've been told by one of my son's assisting doctors, Dr. Stephen Berkiwitcz, you don't even have a medical degree. You're just some quack parading around selling snake oils and charms and boosting the hopes of stricken people while scamming them, taking their money, and producing no results. Admit it. Isn't that correct, Dr. Larsons, or should I simply call you Val?"

The near-chocolate-complexioned woman looked at Audrey with somewhat saddened brown eyes, then spoke, "It is true, Miss Campbell. I was dismissed after failing the medical boards three times. Although I did attend medical college for five years, I know I'm wrong, and I should have addressed you and your son truthfully. Yet, Miss Campbell, the field of medicine should be looked at as an endless possibility of wide ranging cures. If we look strictly at the narrow-minded, tunnel-visioned, conventional method from which we've been programmed to view medicine, we may never find a definite cure for many of the diseases that ail the populace. Conventional medicine is founded in the treatment of symptoms and temporary cures. The 'take two aspirin and call me in the morning' logic. My Center for Alternative Medicine deals with the holistic approach."

Audrey, looking at Dr. Larsons in complete bewilderment, asked, "Wha . . . what did you say?"

Dr. Larsons, now walking slightly ahead, broached her real objective. "You see, Miss Campbell, the holistic doctrine is, simply stated, that all bodies—humans, animals, and all organisms such as plants and trees—are comprised of the same thing. Before the advancing of technology, a long time before the industrial revolution, the science of medicine wasn't just reserved for herbs and mudpacks. Other forms of medicine were vastly explored and millions of people survived untold hardships and suffering."

Audrey, with a frightened look in her eye, paused in midstride and retorted, "Wait a minute! Back in those days, they also used witchcraft and black magic!

"I—look, Miss Campbell, I'm not saying that all areas related to medicine—for instance, witchcraft—are all good or provide positive results. What I am saying is that out of the thousands of cases requiring medical treatment, there were some reported cases of complete remission of certain ailments."

"What? Woman, you are crazy? Those doctors were correct in labeling you a 'voodoo priestess'!"

Dr. Larsons raised her voice an octave higher and proclaimed, "If the cure dictates that I need to perform voodoo, then I will do just that. Now must I remind you that voodoo is a common practice founded in the roots of the South during slavery, derived from the many tribes of our African homeland?"

Audrey, dismissing her, said, "Oh, sister, don't you give me none of your black awareness speeches now!"

Audrey now walked ahead as Dr. Larsons followed.

"Listen, Miss Campbell, during the slave era we weren't cared for by doctors. We only had herbalists, people specializing in voodoo, potion gatherers, witchcraft . . . whatever, to cure our illnesses. Now, I'm not totally resigned to using these methods as a whole. But I do combine them with my skills in traditional medicine, along with a monitored plan of healthy foods and exercise."

Audrey sharply turned around, pointed her finger at Dr. Larsons, and said, "And it was that healthy exercise you prescribed that nearly killed my son, one of the doctors said."

"Listen, it increased his heart rate a bit, but any therapist will tell you daily mobility is essential for the well-being of the entire body. It's called exercise, Miss Campbell, and with patterned daily regimens, it's been proven to promote a healthy body and stronger confidence in mind along with—"

Audrey, determined to get rid of Dr. Larsons, said, "Lady, you are a quack! You just stay away from my child and me! You hear me?"

Dr. Larsons, beseeching Audrey to hear her out, lightly touched Audrey's shoulder in an effort to appeal. "Listen, Miss Campbell, quite naturally you've been raised to follow what the traditional medical doctors say, but believe me, there's a whole stockpile of medicine out there that the snooty medical community is unwilling to touch yet. Just look what has sprung up over the past thirty years. You have herbalists, therapists, nutritionists, palmists, astrologists, numerologists, and others. Who knows whether the medical sector is afraid or just plain stupid and resigned to keeping its head in the sand?

"I do know my Center for Alternative Medicine is considered in their eyes as a form of competition. First off, my services are astronomically cheaper than theirs, which is the primary reason they've attempted to close me down on several occasions. Second, I'm more accessible, given that all the doctors practically abandoned and moved out of the inner city due to malpractice insurance rates, crime, and the pursuit of big money. Third, I'm considered an aid to people who can't afford traditional medical care. Fourth, I provide a helpful alternative for people who have exhausted all hope through traditional medicine. And lastly—which is the main reason—I rattle the doors of conventional medicine. I deliver positive results, even sometimes after their methods fail."

"What? By sorcery and magic?"

"If need be, yes. If it provides a cure, then yes. These alternative perspectives shouldn't totally be out of the question. Look, Miss Campbell, my only purpose in founding the center is simply to provide an affordable means of medicine to all people who wouldn't be able to afford it in harsh times like these. I have the results from the experiments I've done on Devon and there is a probable 50 percent match. Do you hear me? There's a 50 percent possibility of helping him!"

"Listen here, Dr. Larsons, voodoo priestess or whatever the hell you are, I'm not far removed from being a violent woman at this point, so help me. And if you don't take your hand off my shoulder, you're going to find out if this Center for Alternative Medicine you run is going to have enough 'hocus pocus' to repair your bruises!"

Dr. Larsons timidly let go as Audrey walked off. She then yelled after Audrey, "Miss Campbell, please be flexible on this issue. I can help you. They would have you believe that heart surgery was learned and perfected in the last thirty years or so, but they fail to tell you it was practiced, and probably mastered, in ancient Egypt some thousands of years before Christ. It's reserved thinking such as this that short changed Dr. Charles Drew's life, a pioneer in blood plasma, who ironically died on the operating table, because they refused to perform a simple blood transfusion on a black man at the time. Miss Campbell, please listen to me!"

Audrey, increasing her distance, shouted back, "You're lucky I don't sue you for malpractice myself after your tricks. Now you just leave us alone!"

The short walk to work had seemingly taken her forever, but she finally made it to her place of employment—late.

Standing by the punch clock in a taunting disposition, tapping his index finger on his wristwatch, was Kasam Nadir, the young manager of Big Motor City Market. He'd had his eye on Audrey for a long while, but because she staunchly refused all his advances, he began to become bitter and it showed, as his last few advances carried foul sexual connotations.

Audrey was fortunate. Aside from having a part-time job, she was also the only neighborhood resident employed at the Arab-owned store. Audrey was considered a hard worker by the owner, Azid Nadir, an older gentleman who believed in the old ways and found it hard at times to adjust to a different country with such a different culture. Yet, he was respectful, cordial, and nice, which was why his customers enjoyed doing business with him.

For many, like the elderly and aid recipients, Azid was known for running a modest tab for them in the final week of the month where ends are hard to meet until their assistance checks arrive. And sadly, Azid's was the only market within a three-mile radius. All the major chain markets had closed down and shipped out a long time ago, and now to even consider reopening shop in the inner city would be deemed a financial disaster.

Audrey possessed only a high school diploma and was finding that in order to make ends meet, she had to also work two nights a week as an exotic dancer at a go-go bar called Martin's. She aspired to become a medical assistant and was attending community college two nights a week. So in essence, with the care her son Devon required, her life was full and couldn't take anymore strain. Despite Audrey's early morning look, she was intriguingly attractive and met quite a number of men as cashier at the market, many of whom tried convincing her to date. But she considered their intentions no different than Kasam's or the flirtations of the one-track-minded bar customers where she moonlighted. It was a matter of record that many of the male patrons of the Big Motor City Market knew she was a dancer at Martin's, and Kasam, more than likely tipped off, used that dart as justification to propel his barrage of sexual innuendos and other harassment.

But she still found the strength to carry on from words of wisdom passed on from the women in her past. The tribulations in a black woman's existence are never accurately assessed. So she just shouldered the burden.

And contrary to what the majority of people surrounding her were led to believe, her mind was not always focused on her situation and despair. She found what could best be described as a "peculiar admiration" for a certain gentleman who shopped at the market every Wednesday. He was more of the quiet, soft-spoken, well-mannered type. He appeared intelligent and possessed a wide array of technical skills as well.

Once, at her cash register, he noticed her intermediate algebra text. He expressed an interest in algebra, then showed her how she could break down a complex algebraic equation using the quadratic formula, which earned her a B+ on her take-home mid-term exam. During another visit, he explained the mechanical and electrical inner workings of her cash register, and one Wednesday even advised Azid on faulty wiring that was dangling from the ceiling near his freezer, presenting an electrical fire-trap, and explained how a simple method of rewiring could correct it. Audrey also admired his courteous demeanor. He was always pleasant and patient with the other customers. He had assisted the elderly Mrs. Beasley time after time by stacking her produce onto the counter, and he helped out a young child or two who was a nickel or dime short. He once refused to allow a mother of three to put back items from her basket, donating his own money, because she had overestimated the amount of food stamps she had.

Even Wednesdays when he didn't really talk to her, he would still speak in that soft-spoken voice of his. "Hello, Miss Campbell, hope your day will be easy."

After a while as part of his weekly shopping excursion, he'd always pay for his last item, which was always a single piece of produce, usually a peach, and present it to her, saying, "Here, I picked the best one in the whole state for you."

As time proceeded, they struck up minimal conversations, starting with the weather, then toward current events in the daily newspaper, next on to their likes, dislikes, and similarities. Audrey couldn't help but notice how they were beginning to become "chummy." Then she didn't see him for a few consecutive Wednesdays. After the second Wednesday, at store closing, she became worried. But after a month's absence, he appeared in the middle of the baked goods section across from her register and asked her out on a dinner date.

Surprised and without as much as a second thought, she blurted out, "Yes." Then she found herself numb, unable to say a thing.

From the man's look, whose name was Aaron Davis (that much she knew), he appeared numb and shocked as well as he casually walked toward her register. He handed her a peach, his money, and a pleasant smile, then exited out the automatic doors.

One thing always leading to another, Audrey had never found time to think about dating with caring for Devon and the constant consultations and monitoring of his condition with doctors, hospitals, and medical staff. Juggling both jobs and school, she was plain exhausted and uninterested in developing a relationship that could possibly involve an emotional or physical commitment. But Aaron, in a most gentlemanly way, brought it to her attention from time to time.

He was modest, but wouldn't let up about their first date and kept asking with the determination of a bill collector expecting payment of an overdue bill. Through neighborhood talk, he had learned about her situation and of her son, Devon. He also knew that Devon was his best friend's master. At times, Aaron found it remarkable that by his having become entangled in Robbie's life, he, Audrey, Devon, and Robbie all unknowingly shared an intimate bond of some kind. This thought gave Aaron a feeling of secret delight and it made him wonder what fate might have in store for them all.

Presently, Audrey was busy ringing up Miss Beasley's groceries. Miss Beasley was a poor elderly woman whose Medicaid papers were tied up in a confused mess (strictly not of her doing), so she was unable to receive glasses. It was just over a year to date that Miss Beasley had befriended a stray cat, and it was usually the topic of her discussions. She continued her chattering until Audrey, surprised, interrupted her in mid-sentence.

"Miss Beasley, are you aware you have a box of condoms in your groceries?"

"Oh dear, how did that get in there?" she said, picking the box up. "You mean to tell me these aren't denture fixtures?"

"Wait right here, Miss Beasley. I'll be right back!"

If Audrey had not been on the register and had been doing inventory, she would have personally done Miss Beasley's shopping for her. Miss Beasley, also somewhat deaf, continued talking to an empty register, wearing down the patience of the other customers who were behind her in line.

Unfortunately, Audrey had to pass by the manager's check station, which was directly beneath the over-the-counter medicine rack. Watching her approach, Kasam leaned over the counter to ensure his comment was heard.

"I docked you fifteen minutes for being five minutes late. Next time, it will be a half hour!"

Audrey, displaying little concern for Kasam, was more worried about the growing line at her register. Finding the item, she rushed back to ring up more groceries.

"Miss Beasley, you've got the highest-priced box of detergent we sell."

"Oh dear, now let me see." After a brief inspection, she said, "Oh mercy me, this isn't instant oatmeal? Heavens child, my eyes are bad. Now do you believe that weatherman last night saying we are supposed to get three inches of snow?"

To the displeasure of many waiting customers, Audrey, taking a breath, rushed out to find Miss Beasley some instant cereal.

* * *

Inside Audrey's apartment, Devon and Robbie lay asleep. Devon's situation was more desperate than it appeared, for not only did he have a nearly complete kidney shutdown, he was also stricken with congenital heart disease and Ewing's Sarcoma, a rare form of cancer affecting his left femur. His multitude of ailments had somehow included a suppressed growth hormone, so even though he was twelve, he had the physical appearance of a five-year-old. The primary concern of his team of physicians was his kidney failure, but since he was presently connected to a life support machine, this concern had taken a temporary seat to the rear. Now, the physicians were chiefly interested in his cancer, which at first was centralized and contained with chemotherapy. However, at present, the cancer had astoundingly replicated, destroying all normal healthy bone marrow cells and converting the femur into a dead husk. Robbie stirred to the sound of a key playing at the outer door lock, and by the click of the lock and a slow squeal of the door knew it was Pamela Williams, the attendant care nurse who was making her routine checkup. Softly opening the bedroom door, she breezed over him, checking the instruments. After the inspection met her satisfaction, she took off her coat, hat, and scarf. She looked over at Robbie, whose tired eyes met hers.

Slowly moving his head up for attention, he flicked his tail, slowly thumping the bed several times in greeting. She petted him on the head while he sniffed her sleeve.

"Nice to see a friendly old face again, Robbie. Now, you know if Ms. Campbell sees you on this bed, she's going to pitch a fit."

Robbie, after receiving his greetings, licked her hand once then returned to his original position before her arrival, lying lackadaisically with his face resting on his outstretched paws.

"Okay, ignore me if you want . . ." She letting out a hiss of wind like a snake. "It's your funeral."

Ms. Williams sat in a chair beside Devon and Robbie and recorded her daily findings. Afterwards, she kicked back, relaxing with a good book until noon. At noon, she prepared two meals, one for Devon and one for Robbie, while she brown-bagged it.

* * *

A few hours passed. Aaron nearly forgot his appointment at the Employment Security Commission with a counselor to discuss his employment possibilities. He made it on time but waited for two and a half hours for the counselor to tell him in a roundabout way what he already knew: "Nothing appears to be available at the present time for your occupational listing. I'm rescheduling you an appointment in sixty days to hopefully see if anything will turn up. Until then, check your newspaper want ads or privately owned employment agencies, perhaps."

How many times had Aaron heard that "prerecorded" message from the various counselors he'd seen here through the years? Deep down, he had really given up any kind of hope of finding a real job, but still he came. For what purpose, he didn't really know. He fantasized, once or twice, of how a counselor would spring up upon his arrival and yell, "Where have you been? We've looked all over for you. We've been holding this incredible paying job that just meets your specific qualifications! Of course, you'll have to relocate out of Detroit into the Sunbelt. There's a hefty fringe benefit package, including insurance, hospitalization, paid vacations and sick leave, free dental and optical care, and unlimited perks like company-paid housing and your own personal car." Yet, as he walked back down the city streets, he rationalized that even he was allowed a dream every now and again.

As he walked with his head to the ground, he couldn't help but remember a familiar tune that spun in his head from time to time, which was also his high school graduation song. A song that, for him, had religious lyrics and would seem strange to passersby if they heard it uttering from his lips. Yet he hummed the song, by Earth, Wind and Fire, titled, "Keep Your Head to the Sky." Unknown to him, a police car made a wide U-turn to pull slowly behind him.

A white and black officer team pulled alongside him and the black officer spoke. "Mister Aaron Davis, or is it Mr. Smooth? How's it been going? Been almost a year now since I last captured you." Officer Darryl Price, and former junior high school classmate of Aaron's, continued, "Heard there's been a number of burglaries in the precinct. Guess you wouldn't know anything of it?"

Price's partner, Officer Jason Ranietti, slumped down into his seat to take a gander at Aaron's face.

"Nope, I wouldn't know about that or any breaking and entering. I've been straight, as you can see . . ." gesturing to the Employment Commission. "That's the only place I've been doing my "entering" and it's during regular daylight hours. The only thing "breaking" lately been my heart after coming out of that place still unemployed."

"Ha, ha," officer Ranietti laughed. "You're a smart one." Their car radio switched in with static, reporting on a "shots fired," police call in the neighborhood.

Officer Ranietti, now serious, said, "We better respond as backup for that!"

Officer Price agreed, then gave Aaron a careful look. "Okay, 'Smooth,' we'll talk later. And just be warned, we'll be rotating to midnights soon, so I most definitely expect my precinct to be clear of any B and E's on my shift!"

Aaron gave a half smile, then cleverly spoke, "Then I'll say a prayer for you, my son."

Price grunted, "Let's get outta here!"

Aaron continued walking his path, then after a block or two he resumed humming the song.

* * *

Audrey returned home. Walking into her son's room, she saw Ms. Williams reading in a chair and Robbie stretched out on the floor. He looked up at her.

"Hello, Pamela, how are you doing?"

"Just fine."

Audrey walked over to her son, bent over and gave him a long hug and kiss, and spoke briefly to him. She stood up, her eyes meeting Robbie's with a look of disgust. "Tell me, Pam, has this walking flea motel been lying on my son's bed?"

"Well, ah-h," Pamela stuttered as she began picking up charts. "Miss Campbell, I've noticed your son's life signs over the past few months have improved with such positive results. Look!"

Irritated, with her eyes still locked on Robbie, Audrey switched moods, eager to follow Pamela's cheerful lead. "Is that so?" she smiled. "I knew my baby could do it!"

Three or so hours passed and Audrey had prepared dinner, showered, and was out the door for her medical assistant classes. After an hour and a half elapsed, like clockwork, Robbie began scratching on the walls, attempting to get Miss Ford's attention next door. She was the babysitter. As he scratched for ten minutes with still no sign of her, he hoped she wasn't watching another one of those slash-and-gore movies that she loved so much. Many times the oversexed teenager's shrieks had become so loud and frequent that his pawing sounds would go unnoticed.

Eureka! he thought as he heard her tiny feet, with the weight of her small, pudgy, round body hitting the wooden floor and fumbling with the door locks.

"Just a minute, will you? Just a minute! Why, it never fails. It's a conspiracy, I think. You must sit and wait to interrupt me on the good part, just so you can raise a leg to the fire hydrant." She opened the door with the spare key Audrey had entrusted to her to look after Devon, as well as for this specific purpose.

Robbie stuck his head out the door, looking around the corner in Old Man Honeycutt's direction, then looked up to her to ascertain if it was safe.

"The coast is clear already! Did you think I'd sit here and tell you it was when it wasn't?"

Robbie peeped around the corner once more then darted quickly toward the stairs and out the basement window. Later, after the first call of nature, the relief of simple bodily functions completed, he sniffed the cold night air and tried determining what pastime would be on tonight's agenda. While sniffing the ground and the corner of a building, he struck up an idea. *I know. I haven't seen the Sanchez family for a while now for a handout.*

Turning around, he crossed the street, walking through familiar yards and between houses. Along the way, he sniffed various hedges, trees, and sides of homes. Robbie loved this time of the night. With the cold breeze in his face parting his fur, he felt free, floating on the wind currents like a bird; he felt as though he could fly—fly along the clouds, right alongside them. Glancing up at a passing seagull that drifted with ease above him, cawing in a low tone with seemingly not a care in the world, Robbie believed it became part of the wind. He thought there could be no greater feeling than being among their kind, floating free and soaring high on the currents of the breeze.

As he walked through the night's city streets, he heard an occasional dog bark in the distance, which would volley with other dogs barking. This "drumbeat" of communication was similar to the human version of the eleven o'clock news. Listening to the drumbeat, he learned that Dixie and T-Rex fought another battle. There was a shouting match as to who was the exact winner. Elsewhere, Piper, who usually allowed relaxed passage through his yard, now strictly enforced a no-entrance warning.

Humph, Robbie thought. *Must got some juicy bones buried back there somewhere.*

Lancelot was getting stir-crazy again being chained to his doghouse, as usual. Once every three weeks, he'd weaken the new chain bought to restrain him and it would snap. Then he'd spend a couple nights on the town. Robbie hung with him once or twice on his excursions after his "prison break." Lancelot, a

Bouvier, was quite fun at times; however, being incarcerated had a rather strange effect on a dog, compared to one who was simply allowed to wander—and it showed. Lancelot appeared more reckless and gutsier than most. Robbie found himself being Lancelot's chaperon rather than a rebel-rousing cohort. Always after spending a night on the town with him, Robbie found himself feeling more pooped than rejuvenated or satisfied.

Hmm, a newsbreak. It seems Louie the Third is cautioning a would-be passerby near his property to do just that. Now, Trixie and Marcus are doing likewise. Well, he appears not to be a troublemaker. That's good news. It seems like the same old news to me; nothing really changes.

Robbie walked carelessly across a main street that he wouldn't normally walk on with such a lack of concern during the day due to its usual concentration of traffic. In the middle of the road, he wisely awaited the passing of two buses and made his approach onto the remaining lane of the street. He determined by the timid driving style of the approaching vehicle that he could cross in front of it with a minor degree of caution. Walking right into the path of the approaching car as if ignoring it, he crossed in front of it while the driver blew his horn and screamed a profanity or two at him. Robbie, now on the sidewalk, turned his head to give the still shouting driver, who blocked the roadway, a look. "Sure", Robbie yelled. "You're tough now", shouting behind two thousand or so pounds of heavy steel, "but if you were out from behind that wheel on the street with me here now, I'd be the one chewing your rear out!"

Robbie walked on, crossing another street. He walked on the sidewalk for three blocks, then trailed his nose, fishing along the gutter, hoping to luck up on a trashed morsel or the scent of a new dog in the territory. At an intersection, another car blew its horn at him while attempting to make a right turn. Robbie, caught by surprise, jumped onto the sidewalk as the teenagers yelled at him and blew their horn constantly.

Uh-oh, youngsters mean trouble.

The deep bass from the audio equipment blaring outside the car should've been warning enough. Now Robbie found himself dancing to avoid the aim of a daring teenager with an empty beer bottle while the boy's companions cheered him on. Dodging the youngster's aim from the car, Robbie displayed a look of scared uncertainty. Then he finally stood still and waited. The boy sent another bottle with a crash, hailing three feet over Robbie's head. His companions groaned with displeasure.

Robbie watched them as they sped off. *You can always tell the Little League pitching dropouts ... with that arm, that kid better keep his day job flipping burgers at White Castle where he belongs.*

Robbie walked through a course of thick bushes that sprouted inside a vacant lot and enjoyed his second favorite pleasure—the scratching and combing effect the bushes had as they coursed the entire length of his body. He loved the tingly effect it gave traversing his skin. It took him back to when he was still a puppy and an owner he could barely remember used to give him a good, thorough brushing from time to time. He seldom wondered about that one-time owner.

Strolling through the Sanchez's yard, he climbed their back porch and scratched insistently on their door. Waiting patiently, he looked beyond the yard, back onto the streetlight-lit foreground. A man was trying to snare a cab and ran after it blindly, unable to see the paying fare in the rear.

A bagman, who he scarcely remembered, sifted longingly through a refuse basket.

Robbie scratched again, even after hearing Mrs. Sanchez mumble she was coming. He could probably guess by the whirl of the electronic can opener that she was busy preparing his food. Yet at times, he knew playing "dumb dog" could prove beneficial. Mrs. Sanchez called out to her husband and her two children to greet him and turned on the back porch light. Robbie—or Jessie as they'd named him—wasn't too thrilled at having an audience watch him while he ate, but he figured that entertainment was the least he could pay them for a meal, besides an added bark or two. (This thrilled the kids.) And "Jessie" knew how to thrill the kids.

Mrs. Sanchez opened the door to Robbie wagging his tail as she placed his bowl before him. Giving him a gentle pat, she giggled as the two children screamed in delight to watch him eat. He gobbled the canned dog food down quickly, and Mrs. Sanchez gave him a dish of water and petted him again gently, calling out to the two children, "Mira, Enrique. Mira, Sondrique." Coaxed on by their mother, both children timidly petted him. Then, with a rush of excitement and sharp giggles, they ran to hide behind the safety of their mother. Mrs. Sanchez again called out to her husband.

He called back, "¿Que paso?"

"En la cocina, ¡pronto!"

Mr. Sanchez walked to the door, carefully holding a small bundle. Robbie thought, as he watched the delicate, painstaking way Mr. Sanchez carried the bundle, that he could have been carrying a small crate of eggs. He introduced the bundle to Robbie as Pepito.

Robbie looked at the still-closed eyes of the small one nestled in the bundle as Mr. Sanchez leaned down for him to take a closer look. *Hmm, kid, so you want some advice, huh? Well it's a cold, hard world out here, as you probably can't see right now. Just work hard, like both your parents do at school, and you'll do well in this life. That's practically the only advice I could give to a young one such as yourself.*

Next, in response to Mr. Sanchez's request to speak ("Jessie, ¡habla!"), he barked several times to the children's delight and shrill shouts of, "¡otra vez!" Robbie did indeed know how to work the kids. During the course of his life, children had always been instrumental and the most susceptible to his well-staged acts of heart-wrenching pity. Initially, he would lead them on with the playful puppy act—fetching a ball, rolling over, or extending a paw in a handshake. If that didn't work, he would simply tag along behind them for days on end, accompanying them everywhere they would go until they became fond of his presence. Finally, if not lured by his charm, he'd pull from his arsenal his all ensnaring "smart weapon"—the saddened display of the watery, long-eyed, puppy-dog look. It was a safe bet that if one didn't get them, usually the other would.

As Robbie walked the distance home, temporarily losing his breath to the exhaust fumes of a bus as it roared by, he thought about the main question that had been plaguing his mind for a number of years. Why? Why, for the life of him, was he so attracted to Devon? And better yet, vice versa. Why was Devon attached to a wandering vagabond tramp such as him?

At first, Robbie thought it best left unexplained; however, it was a unique bond that he shared with Devon, unlike his bond with Aaron. He couldn't understand it, but he knew the first time they'd happened onto each other that the bond they established felt like fate—like it was ordained. There was a strange aura that seemed mystical about their meeting. It drew them together—solidified them.

It was later, after making it back to the floor where Devon's apartment resided, that he sat at the end of the hall, waiting in long suspense. Mr. Honeycutt's door was ajar.

So, he patiently waited the several hours in the stairwell until Mr. Honeycutt's door was firmly closed and locked. The night unfolded into the day, as the day's results fared much the same as they had the day before.

However, on this night it was Robbie's primary duty to watch Audrey from afar, exiting from her night job, and to see her safely board a cab. After that it was Miss Ford's duty, upon receiving a call, to stand in the window awaiting Audrey's arrival and to see her safely into the apartment. And for Robbie it was nothing unusual. Nothing but the long walk home.

The next morning was Wednesday. Audrey nearly forgot, since she always tried to put on something a little more special on Wednesdays. Something she had never really worn before on this special day of the week. She also found that on this day she would spend more time in the mirror, putting on makeup and teasing her hair. Upon her arrival to work, she was five minutes early; however, she observed an unusual smirk on Kasam's face. She would usually ignore a smirk by him, but there was something uncommonly sinister about this particular smirk. However today was Wednesday, and practically no one—but Devon—was entitled to mess up her only day of feeling truly valued as a lady.

It was near closing when Aaron approached. The tall, lean-framed, light-brown-skinned man walked inside the store, looking to her like a gallant knight in shining armor. The basket he whisked away with ease by one hand was like him guiding a gigantic steed he masterfully rode. Attempting to not be too obvious, she tried concentrating on the groceries she was ringing up, but she couldn't help constantly looking up to follow his movements from one row to the next. He quickly shopped.

Momentarily losing herself, one of the female patrons was quick to caution her, "Hey, ahh, ahh, watch it, girlfriend. You just charged me four times for this one can. Now, I know he looks good, but to me, he ain't worth the price of four cans of salmon!"

Audrey, feeling embarrassed seeing the mistake printed right on the paper receipt, said, "Oh, I'm awfully sorry. Here, I won't charge you for the meat. That'll give you a discount on your total food bill," she whispered.

The woman's eyes bucked, then she spoke. "Shoot, I wanna shop here every day that man shops here. That man's good luck!"

Audrey carefully counted out her change and handed it to the woman while she hypnotically looked up.

"Hey, what's the four-digit number for 'handsome man bearing good luck'?" the woman then asked.

"I don't know," Audrey spoke, staring off into the distance.

Aaron, coincidently, was the last customer. Audrey, coming to her senses, shook herself. *Am I going crazy?* she thought. *What's coming over me? It's like I've totally forgotten my pledge!*

Aaron approached her as he spoke, "Hello, Miss Campbell, you're looking very beautiful today. That red bow in your hair sure is a cute touch. Well here it is, the finest one in the whole

state," he said, handing her a peach. Then swinging it away from
her outstretched hand, he added, "But it definitely can't match
your beauty!" Handing it to her gently as their eyes met, he said,
"Here, I picked it especially for you."

Did time suddenly stop? she wondered. For her, it felt as
though they were the only two people in the world.

Kasam watched as always, with a bird's-eye view from his
manager's perch.

The couple talked for a while, finally agreeing upon their
date for a day next week.

"Audrey, it's time you turned in your drawer!" Kasam
shouted, practically going unnoticed.

Audrey's reply was a simple wave of her hand. Azid, closing
up the rear office, noticed the couple. Standing in the doorway, a
warm feeling overcame him while he observed the two. He smiled.

Aaron, knowing the high sign to leave, said, "Okay, so our
date is sealed." Looking at her endearingly, he spoke softly, "Until
I see you next week. 'Bye."

And then he did it. He probably didn't know he did it, but he
did it. He went and gently placed his warm, soft hand on hers,
which was minding its own business face down on the counter.
That did it!

Why did he go and do that? she thought. Her legs, like whittled down matchsticks, awaited his departure to break. *What
am I doing?* She thought. *Oh, why am I doing this? What about my
pledge?* Gathering herself, she finally turned in her cash drawer.

* * *

Miles away, inside of the Center for Alternative Medicine,
another woman was coping differently with her ending day's
work, as Dr. Val Larsons leaned tiredly over her obstructed
desktop filled with files. Her door slowly opened and she looked
up. It was her nurse.

"Please, JeNitra, unless it's an emergency, no more patients,
please."

"It's Mr. Phillips. He's complaining about his back."

"Tell him he'll be my first patient tomorrow morning."

"He says he's in great pain, Doctor."

Dr. Larsons sighed. "Okay. He'll have to wait ten or fifteen minutes. Meanwhile, clear out the lobby. If anyone else is there, schedule them for appointments first thing in the morning."

"All right, Doctor."

The doctor, straightening her files in her drawer, now pulled out the file on Devon Campbell. Thumbing through the pages of his file, as she had many times before, she ran across a data page on his dog, Robbie. She had noticed the close kinship between the boy and the dog, and it had jostled ideas in her head—ideas about certain probabilities. She held up a copy of a letter she had personally typed, which she was now used to seeing, but she was truthfully a little dismayed that it had received no response.

Elsewhere, another letter was being written:

```
Dr. Stephen Berkiwitcz
Professor of Biochemical Studies
Director of Research
Stockwell University
Ashdown, Arkansas


Dr. Durell Saunders
Professor of Microsurgery,
Fisk University School of Medicine—Medical
Studies

Re: Devon Campbell and Test Subject A

My Dear Colleague,

First off, I would like to extend my congratula-
tions to you on your fine paper and dissertation
```

to the Alumni of Scholar Medical Scientists at Morehouse College of Medicine last spring. I was among the many scholars in the audience. Believe it or not, we've met once before. I know this might have passed your desk sometime ago; however, I can't help but notice the intriguing raw data this report discloses. Looking at it yourself, perhaps a doctor of your stature will find the information from these many pages that I have submitted to you interesting at best, but as the reports document, the patient has an almost zero compatibility with all closest family members, and outside family matches have proven zero. Yet, Test Subject A provided a 30 percent Probable Compatibility Acceptance Rate (PCAR) for bone transplantation.

Now, I don't want to sound like some touched, scientific-reality-stretching scientist from some bad B grade movie off a late-night channel, but in comparing this amazing data with my own field of testing, I was quite stunned—like you at this moment, reading this—but now I caution you to prepare yourself. (This is the part you might want to sit down for!) Most of my information, which prompts such a far-fetched study, was from Dr. Val Larsons, the head of the Center for Alternative Medicine based in Detroit. (This broken branch of medicine, for some who may want to remotely associate with it, is rumored to dabble in the likes of snake oils and charms). I know now I've probably lost your interest and you've dismissed me as that lunatic quack from above, yet bear with me if you will. This is cold, hard data that I have received, tested, and proven, as my notes will show.

Now what if this PCAR does indeed hold true and a successful transplant was performed? Please, don't get me wrong. I'm well familiar from my two terms of comparative anatomy and physiology classes in undergrad (and I must testify, I've slept through a few sessions). However, an operation of this magnitude would generate the moving force needed to push that huge boulder rolling down the hill and into the valley of those stiff-shirted, old-timer medical board members. I myself would personally love to witness the steam rising from their ever-doubtful heads. If the transplant is completed and has just a six-day immunological acceptance rate, it would be considered a success in medical terms.

I'm aware this transplant in reality is doomed for failure and has ridicule written all over it, but you could imagine the notoriety gained from such an endeavor if it reached fruition. An endeavor of humane interest foremost, of course, yet can you imagine the proponents of its aftermath? Now, I know the cost of such a task may prove beyond reach, along with the number of man-hours to be put in. So here's where my second favor comes in (the first was reading this letter). As you can see in the preceding pages of the information I've sent to you, I've contacted a wide range of experts in the field of medicine, including Dr. Danker Voltheim, the visiting premiere surgeon in veterinary medicine, compiling my list and requesting that they donate their time foremost and money if possible. My constituents and I have been banging the drums of contribution on the street corners of the medical sector for this cause.

I hope that you will consider such a venture amongst some of the best of your fellow colleagues. Your expertise in transplants and microsurgery has been noted the world over, and I find it a tribute that a former Detroiter who has gained such acceptance could prove positive results with lending a helpful hand.

Also, if I failed to mention the urgent human element that's at stake here, the pendulum swings for the life of our patient who is twelve years old. I pray that your busy timetable and any thoughts to the contrary would yield to compromise in alliance of our initiative.

Until we meet again on the back nine, stuck in that horrible quicksand they call a sand trap at Florida's Pebble Lake golf course, I bid you good science.

Dr. Stephen Berkiwitcz
Stockwell University

* * *

It was a little later than usual as Robbie left that evening. He had decided to wait for Devon to fall soundly asleep before he departed, bolting out the door and slightly startling Miss Ford as she opened it, who had been shaken over a George Romero movie.

Robbie, pleased to be getting out into the fresh cool air, sat for a moment, taking it all in. He had looked forward to tonight, since tonight was the night for hanging with the gang. Speaking of gang, off in the distance, several blocks from where he sat, he heard a bark that belonged to one of the members. Along with the nagging bark, every so often he would hear the screech of tires.

"For Fido's sake! When will this dog ever learn?" Robbie broke off into an urgent, full run down the block. Springing to attention at the beginning of the next block was Nephertiti, a picture-perfect Afghan hound with owners who always trimmed, bathed, and debugged her regularly. She was sitting on the porch, up on all fours yelling out, "Robbie, where are you running off to? I thought we—"

"No time for that. Just come on! Our Toby's at it again!"

Nephertiti, now running, exclaimed, "Oh no! How many times do we have to tell him?"

"Obviously, we'll have to forever. Or up until he's dead. Whichever comes first!"

Nephertiti's owners, although they pampered her with the best (at least better than most of the dogs in the neighborhood), let her exercise her freedom to go out for a while now and then. Robbie had to admit that he'd had reserved thoughts about her back when he first met her, but after getting to know her, he found out how very wrong those preconceived thoughts were of her. In his mind, Nephertiti was the most down-to-earth canine he had ever met.

Turning around the corner toward all the ruckus, Robbie saw Toby chasing behind a car and yelled out, "Come back here, you doofus! Any mutt'd know chasing after cars is dangerous. That leisure trend played out a long time ago. Besides, sniffing up behind vehicle exhaust is hazardous to your health!"

The car screeched its tires to a dead stop as the driver screamed at the top of his lungs out of the window, "Why, you four-legged imbecile! What the heck's wrong with you? I would get outta my car and brain ya if you had any sense in that stupid dog skull of yours!"

Toby stood in all his glory, still argumentatively barking at the car and driver. Robbie and Nephertiti, from about fifty feet away, yelled at Toby to listen to them and cease his activity. But no, not Toby; he was still barking stubbornly at the car.

The man then yelled, "It's lucky for you I always believed in being kind to dumb animals—" Suddenly, the three dogs saw the car's gears switch to reverse as the rear taillights flashed brightly. "But stupid animals, that's a whole different thing!"

"Uh-oh, Toby, we're all in trouble. You better run for your life!" Nephertiti shouted.

Nephertiti and Robbie ran. Toby finally stopped barking after seeing the tires spinning wildly in reverse towards him. He began fleeing in retreat like the others, finding temporary safety in an alley. The car still followed them in reverse, but then the driver lost control, crashing into a garbage dumpster. The three escaped, running past the car, out of the alley, and back onto the streets. As they ran further, they could still hear the now dwindling threats of the man yelling in revenge for his wrecked car.

After a severe tongue lashing by both Nephertiti and Robbie, Toby, mainly a Newfoundland mixture, decided to refrain from any more such stunts—for the present time at least. The three dogs walked through the neighborhood, attempting to decide on the night's activity. They turned into another alley and stumbled across Swift Claw, who was foraging in a garbage can.

Now, Swift Claw wasn't just any cat. Swift Claw was an alley cat. She was very noticeable because she was a white longhair with several patches of black fur over her body, with the most distinctive being the patch over her left eye, which gave her an ominous look. It was well known to never approach Swift Claw because of her temperament. Usually you let her greet you first.

"Hey, there's Swift Claw. Let's see if she'll join us," Nephertiti suggested. "She might have an idea on eats! Hey, Swift Claw," she called from a distance as the three dogs halted their approach, awaiting an answer.

Swift Claw slowly looked at the three then poked her head back into the interior of the trashcan as if she hadn't noticed them.

Robbie now spoke, "Hey ya, Swift Claw. What'cha know? We're going somewhere for a bite, care to join us? If not . . . got any suggestions?"

Swift Claw's body suddenly stiffened, but her head still remained in the trashcan.

"Come on, Swifty, why don't you let the cat outta the can and join us?" Toby joked.

Swift Claw stirred the contents inside the trashcan for a few seconds more, then slowly climbed down and stealthily strolled toward the three. Her muted footsteps graced the concrete as she calmly brushed by Nephertiti—which was her arrogant way of greeting them—then by Robbie, who was still unsettled by such an unusual custom, and lastly, by Toby. Almost immediately a lightening claw sliced the air, too fast to see, but its effects were surely felt when it hit its mark.

Toby let out a painful yell. "Yeeeargh!"

As anyone who had even limited contact with her could surely attest, Swift Claw had always been known to be short on temper and long on naps.

Toby, retreating behind the two, muttered, "Ouch, that hurts. Can't cha take a joke?"

Swift Claw, giving him her steady-eyed treatment, glowered as if the question didn't even merit an answer. Swift Claw, a born-and-raised alley cat, a loner, and a devoted warrior in the true sense of the word, stood poised.

Nephertiti spoke up, saying, "We came up with the usual eating spots and we thought you could offer a suggestion and maybe join us—that's, of course, if you're not busy."

Swift Claw, turning her attention from Toby, sat down and began to groom herself. She ceased washing her face for a second to mumble in a low whine, "Purrrr-haps Otto's Fish Market?"

Robbie cringed—somehow knowing that would be her suggestion—and spoke up, first trying not to offend her sensitive mood, "I'm really not up for fish tonight, Swift Claw. Maybe something else?"

Toby agreed, "Yeah. Besides, I never eat that stuff anyway. I just find myself prompted to uncontrollably flop to the ground and rub up against it. Last time, my family kept me outside for two days until the smell left." Speaking quietly under his breath, he added, "Don't see how no silly cat can eat that smelly stuff anyway."

Toby froze in shock to see Swift Claw stop her facial to give him a deadpan look. In trouble again, he retreated even further towards the rear as he looked into her smothering eyes, realizing she had heard what he had whispered.

Nephertiti, trying to block their infighting, said, "Hey, I have an idea. How about Derek's Steak and Lobster House? It's a little out of our area, but the large-portioned leftovers are well worth it."

"Hey, Teetee, now that's a place we've overlooked for some time. Great idea!" Robbie shouted.

Swift Claw, who had returned to cleaning her face, spoke with a low hum, "Purrractically purrrfect!"

"Yeah, good choice," Toby agreed, as the four proceeded, turning from the alley, which was now out of sight.

Robbie said, "Yes, that was indeed an excellent choice, Nephertiti. I must agree ... err ahem, not to say that your Otto's Fish Market was a bad choice there, Swift Claw."

They heard a swat as Toby let out another surprised yelp, then moaned, "It's not healthy to hold a grudge, you frutkussing feline you!"

After a timely journey with Swift Claw slowly bringing up the rear, the four, having converged behind the fenced compound of the restaurant and dined, were settling in now for the post-consumption digestive phase.

Nephertiti, with a stuffed belly, groaned, "I ate too much. I think I've just lost my trim, chic figure."

"The roast was a little dry, but good," Toby commented.

"Well, the steak bone and lamb chops I had were first-rate!" Robbie was glad to announce.

"Mmm, I just love halibut and purrrrch."

The after-meal conversation continued as Swift Claw, reclining at a distance, drifted off to sleep.

"Right now that cool mineral spring water my owner places in my dish from time to time would be the ending cap of a perfect meal," Nephertiti commented.

"I've got that beat—cold water drippings from the hose off of Timothy's Fruit and Vegetable Stand in Eastern Market. Man, those vitamins and nutrients pooling together then washing over into the gutter . . ." Robbie gave a salivating lick. "Nothing could top that refreshing drink."

"Awww, you're both all wet!" Toby commented as he crawled on all fours, closing the three-dog circle they were in, and lazily rolled over onto his side. "The best drink all around on a cool night like this comes straight outta my family's toilet. The water's cool, plentiful, and you never have to worry about one of them pushing you aside for a lap!"

Nephertiti, feeling grossed out, squinted her eyes and stuck her tongue out. "Oh, how could you mention that after such a pleasant meal?"

"Hey, don't knock it if you haven't tried it."

"E-e-e—you!"

"Actually he's got a point there, Teetee. It isn't all that bad."

They continued their conversational bantering back and forth, while completely unnoticed in front of them, blending well within the shadows and having watched the trespassers, three Doberman pinschers walked upon them.

The trio of pals suddenly stood up as silence coursed between the two groups. Robbie calmly spoke in a low voice, "Nephertiti, guard Swift Claw."

She slowly backed up behind Robbie and Toby, never taking her eyes off the now-growling Dobermans as the totally oblivious Swift Claw slept peacefully. Nephertiti was overprotective of Swift Claw because she knew of these hateful types. How they congregate in mobs and the viciousness they inflict on Swift Claw's kind and other weaker animals. She had long considered Swift Claw to be family among their small band and would gladly defend her until the death if need be.

One of the Dobermans spoke, "Whether the dame likes it or not, you're all in the toilet now!"

"What're you doing stepping foot on our property?" another Doberman spoke in a menacing voice as he stepped closer.

Robbie and Toby both growled on the defensive as Robbie spoke, "We meant no harm. We were merely hungry, that's all. We'll leave now. We don't wish any trouble.

"Humph!" the third Doberman spoke. "I smell a coward amongst the ranks. Know what we did to the last two cowards? We took our time ripping them to shreds. There's nothing we hate worse than cowards!"

The second Doberman spoke again. "Besides, we've left markers all around the yard. One of ya had to have smelled the scent. You all willfully trespassed, and now you'll have to pay the price!"

"Look, we are not looking for a fight, but if a fight is what you want, by golly, a fight is what you'll get!" Robbie commenced bearing his fangs, awaiting an attack.

Amid the growls and snarling, a familiar low voice brought silence to both groups, now girded and eager to engage in battle. "Purrr-mit me, my friend," Swift Claw resounded, stepping in front of Nephertiti.

"Well, well, guys, look at what we have here! Now this is what I call a blue light special!" the first Doberman spoke.

The third now speaking, said, "Did I just say there's nothing we hate worst than cowards? Well now, I stand corrected. There's absolutely nothing we hate more than wussy pussies!"

Swift Claw, in her usual crafty manner, strolled coolly over alongside Toby as she whispered smoothly, "Gentlemen, purrr-chance this is nothing worth losing a testicle over?"

The second Doberman looked sheepishly between his legs, then back at her, realizing how she immediately pinpointed their vulnerability.

The third one spoke again. "Never in all my days. We've got an uppity one here. I'm definitely relishing the thought of you paying the price, fur ball. I'm gonna personally gut you clean like those two kittens we caught out back here a week ago!"

The dogs would have ceased laughing had their eyes seen the hair on Swift Claw's back stand on end as if electrically charged. Raising one paw high into the night's air, her fierce claws extended with a harsh flash as it grabbed the Doberman's undivided attention. Swift Claw's back was now fully arched, her ears pinned down and her eyes locked upon the Doberman's. "Mmmm, thissss is a purrr-chase I'd gladly purrr-vide the wet works for, gang!"

Toby, hearing this ominous statement, knew her well and knew that was a clue meant for them to leave, without question. "Come on, let's scram!"

Robbie watched, confused, as Swift Claw stalked the slowly retreating Dobermans who were nervously heading back up a flight of steps. This action gave Toby insight into the expression "lambs being led to slaughter."

Robbie got that same eerie sense and agreed as he backed away. "Okay, Swift Claw, you sure you're gonna be alright?"

Swift Claw ignored him. Her mind honed in on what she was determined to do.

"Maybe she needs our help!" Nephertiti interjected.

Toby, ushering her back, said, "Trust me when I say this: she'll be okay!"

As the dogs left the alley and rounded the corner, they heard the ferocious cry of Swift Claw and the yelping pleas of dogs echoing through the neighborhood.

The three buddies headed home and didn't say much, not until Robbie and Toby walked Nephertiti to her doorstep.

Naturally inquisitive, Nephertiti was the first one to break the ice. "What happened back there with Swift Claw? What made her suddenly snap like that?"

She looked to Robbie, who usually always had an answer, but his face looked just as blank and filled with questions as hers. Then she looked over to Toby for the answer.

Toby at first held it all in, then replied, "Those roughnecks back there struck the wrong nerve with Swift Claw. You see, she had a litter once . . ."

"Swift Claw?" Nephertiti exclaimed in shock.

"Naw, you're joking, right," Robbie giggled disbelievingly, expecting Toby to bowl over, splitting his side from pulling their legs.

But Toby never looked more serious as he continued. "She had a litter of three kittens some time ago. One day she and her young were looking for food over off Warren Avenue, inside that wreckage yard unbeknownst to her at that time they had acquire a pack of guard dogs. Well, anyway, she was lucky to make it out of there alive."

Nephertiti, hanging her head down sadly, said, "I-I-I never knew."

Robbie, still somewhat in disbelief, added, "I never would have thought . . ."

"Yeah, that was a terrible break for Swifty, but it happened and it's in the past." Toby looked up and said, "Hey guys, I gotta go before the mister falls asleep in the lazy chair again watching TV and won't hear me trying to signal him to let me in. I would hate to sleep on the front porch tonight; it looks like it's gonna get real cold."

Nephertiti bade him good-bye. "Hey gang, tonight was a blast. We ought to do this more often."

"Oh, and by the way, about what I told you . . ."

Robbie spoke up, "Don't worry, Toby. Our lips are forever sealed."

They watched as Toby disappeared, sprinting between the houses.

"That was just horrible, a terrible experience. I don't think I would have the courage to survive something like that."

"Don't sell yourself short, Teetee. If you truly had to, you'd find the means."

"I really don't know. I consider my life most fortunate as compared to hers, or even yours for that matter! You having to care for and watch over little Devon—the stress must be unbearable. Wait a minute, why aren't you with him this very minute? I've noticed the past few months you've been slacking, neglecting your duties as a family member. You know how terribly that young boy depends upon you like nobody else. So what gives?"

Robbie looked deep in thought, as if he was just transported to a different world, and asked, "Teetee, do you know what love is?"

Nephertiti, looked puzzled for a second wondering the origin of such a question and answered, "Sure, I guess. It's when you have a deep feeling for someone where you would give up anything for their welfare."

Robbie thought for a spell, then asked another peculiar question. "Do you love your human family?"

She paused thinking it was a trick question. "Why, yes, sure I do. What would make you ask such a question?"

Robbie looked bewildered as he stepped away. His back was to her now. He didn't return an answer to her question, but instead he asked, "Do you have any idea what it's like to slowly die inside?"

Nephertiti, now really shocked, said, "What? What are you talking about?"

"It's nothing," he muttered, then hesitantly ran off.

Nephertiti called out to him, "Robbie, wait! What are you talking about? Come back! Let's talk!" It was too late; he had already escaped out of sight.

After a while of aimless wandering, Robbie sat perched in his runaway hiding spot. It was his beacon of solitude where he collectively did his soul searching. Sitting midway upon a towering metal fire escape that overlooked the Fischer Freeway from the rear of the old dilapidated and gutted Motown recording studio, he watched hundreds of cars travel by. Sitting here for hours at a time with no desire to return home, he thought of this freeway and its purpose. He came up with an idea that to him, in a roundabout way, provided the perfect explanation of life.

Robbie's thoughts rambled as he watched the freeway traffic. *One road, with many lanes flowing in both directions. Sometimes the lanes are filled and then other times not—different humans, ranging in different ages, driving in different cars, some alone, some with various others, all different in attitudes, with different destinations. No two quite the same, all dressed differently; some just getting on, while others exiting. Many do the required speed limit, while others casually take their time with no rush, and then others zip by in a panicked hurry.*

He watched one man who was sidelined, changing a flat tire. In the opposite lane further down, he observed an abandoned car sitting in the emergency lane with its hood up; the car had not been there a few days ago. From time to time, he'd witnessed accidents there, from the mild fender bender to the fifteen-car pileup. Off into the distance, he could see the flashing red globe of a police vehicle, obviously stopping someone for a traffic infraction. It was this unique, pulsing, random, ever-flowing exchange that he grew to rationalize essentially as life.

From this point, he wondered about many things to take his mind off one driving question that subconsciously nagged him. Thoughts such as where had he been, what was to be, when would his life be done, would he be reincarnated as a human traveling around in those rubber spinning metal boxed cars with an agenda? Suddenly, while drowned in thought, it came to him, pulling, nagging at his subconscious. "What could possibly make me feel the way I do?"

He didn't have an answer or any inclination as to the reason why. Could it be he felt guilty? He dealt with month after month of a seemingly never-ending, downward roller coaster ride with

Devon's life signs appearing only to stabilize at best, then slowly sinking to new depths.

Robbie knew that he and Devon were unexplainably linked. At times he felt Devon's pain ripple through the distance, and sometimes Robbie felt more penetrable shock waves by lying beside Devon. Or the most overwhelming, direct eye-to-eye contact, which undeniably caused the worst pain. The majority of times during those encounters, his senses became totally inundated with Devon's. He was there along with him for the ride. He felt powerless, helpless. There were times, when, before entering the apartment building, he sensed Devon was having a really bad day and, in turn, would find a reason to delay his visit.

Lately, this pattern became more frequently compared to a child's seesaw: the more reason he found to avoid Devon, the higher his level of guilt. This inescapable predicament, along with his honest confusion in comprehending this unexplainable emotion called love, had a mind-shattering impact upon him. He was just a mere dog, and it left him feeling hopelessly lost.

In this world that he didn't create, where man appeared superior, he longed for understanding and pleaded for assurance—but he found no comfort, no answers, which was in part what troubled his canine soul. Finally, his mind became so exhausted by so many "what if's" and "what could be's" that he fell asleep there, resting until morning.

* * *

Audrey awakened and dressed, listening impatiently for the sounds of scratching on the door as she teased her hair in the mirror. Waiting longer than she normally would on Robbie, she continuously threw a fit with him in her mind, causing her to angrily mumble just under her breath. Giving up her angry tirade to focus on not being late again, she reached into her top drawer for money; today was a bi-weekly Friday, which meant it was prescription day. This was money that she had to store away from both jobs and government assistance, which she needed to pay for Devon's most expensive prescriptions. She was thankful for the government assistance, for she would have never been able to afford the medical equipment that lined Devon's room. He would have been a permanent resident of some hospital that could not provide the attention she felt her son needed. She gave her son a good-bye kiss and observed him stir ever so slightly. Leaving and heading towards the door, she cursed Robbie's name.

At the Big Motor City Market, a lengthy discussion resurfaced. Kasam and Azid were battling it out after having held this debate twice before in the early morning. Each was determined that the other was overwhelmingly wrong in his views. Azid angrily yelled in the rear office, "You're just jealous 'cause she will have nothing to do with you, because she will not bend to your immoral practices. Like when you wanted to hire that other girl you played with who will!"

"You was wrong. She was better girl—better worker!"

"Better worker for you! But don't pull the wool upon my eyes, Kasam."

"So? But this is different—this is family!"

It was true, and Azid knew with that statement that he had been thrown into a most difficult dilemma. It was fact that Azid's cousin—Kasam's sister—was due to come over from the mother country to relocate in Detroit. Being in a new country, of course, she would need a job, and Azid was the family businessman because he owned a store.

"Something you not know—she did undercharge woman yesterday of food. I sat and I watched, and then with my own ears, that very woman told me she did when she came to the booth to play her lottery."

"So, once is nothing—she's a good, dependable worker."

"So that is what you say, but how many times before she undercharged?"

Azid still dismissed the entire incident.

Kasam continued. "It does not matter, she will be gone soon ..." he said, looking hauntingly at his senior cousin. "Because like saying in America, 'blood is thicker than water.'"

He had Azid in a vise and knew it.

Azid didn't have the heart to just cut Audrey off, yet Kasam's statement was fairly accurate, for in the old ways, immigrant blood lines are considered higher priority than a so-called dedicated worker. But then how would he implement a means of discharging her?

Kasam had already formulated a foolproof plan and discussed it with Azid. Kasam proposed that he stealthily slip fifty dollars from her cash drawer, notify the police of her theft, and they would thereby prosecute her for theft. They would then be justified in firing her.

Azid was furious at such a notion and was hopping mad. Yet, Kasam in his smooth, convincing ways, stood to reason with him.

"My cousin Azid, you are of the old teachings. And if we were of the old country still, it may well be of practice, but now we are of new country with new ideas, new teachings. This is the American way—everything is different here and you must readjust to its teachings or you will fail as a person in life!"

Several hours later, inside a restaurant in a business meeting, Aaron sat at breakfast with Rippy, who wanted to discuss a new job with him. This job had long-range sights of being a wonderful business venture if successfully completed. Rippy, aware of Aaron's specialty in electronics and his craftiness in having defused several burglar alarms on a few jobs, knew that with Aaron's knowledge they could get a foot in the door of a whole new field of crime—high-tech espionage. This new job would be their maiden voyage and, if successfully completed, would arouse enough interest by the backer to launch them in other high-paying fields of risk. They were to break into a newly built corporation called Renaissance Technical Designs Partnership and "liberate" secret technical designs on file and on computer discs, which the backer had conveniently labeled.

Aaron, a little unsure about such a new idea, was leery, however the backer promised four thousand dollars each for their work, with assurance of more to come. Aaron immediately tossed in his proposal again for Robbie's fair cut as a member of the gang. Rippy, never one to give up ground when he was set on something, still flatly refused. "If you think he's so important, why don't you just settle it and give him a 10-percent cut outta your share?"

"I've been doing that anyway. I was right to figure you for not being fair." Aaron never told him that he had stashed away money in a safe-deposit box for Robbie's services in Devon's name.

"Fair? I'm fair enough to give you half on each job, ain't I, when it should be sixty-forty?"

Aaron felt himself becoming riled and decided diplomatically to back down, for he felt that he could argue that same case in his favor for his contributions on each job.

"So, anyway now, we gonna to do this job, or what?"

Aaron, too incensed to speak, merely nodded his head in affirmation, eating the last of his eggs and chewing into a slice of toast.

"Good, then it's all set. All I have to do is get the list and we'll be ready to go on Wednesday."

Aaron, shaking his head in disagreement, was unable to speak with his mouthful.

"What? And why not?"

Aaron, trying to clear his mouth of food, paused, then said, "Got something to do."

"Something to do? Well, that something to do might as well wait. We're talking four thousand apiece here!"

"Nah," Aaron said, shaking his head again. "I said I've got something important to do!"

"Trust me, it can wait. We're talking four t-h-o-u-s-a-n-d dollars!"

"Then I'm out!" Aaron said, abruptly getting up and sliding the chair behind him angrily. As he was about to leave—

"Wait, wait, wait!" Rippy pleaded, grabbing Aaron's arm to prevent him from walking out. "Come on, Smooth, relax. Have a seat. If you say so, I'll just have to convince the interested party to push it back one day. It should be no problem. Here, you didn't even finish your orange juice."

Aaron, sliding the drink back across the table, refused to drink.

"Hey, Smooth, this ain't like you, man. What's eating you? Why you would wanna go and change the plans?"

Aaron knew that if he didn't tell, Rippy'd hound him forever. Sure, he could have told him a lie, but with Rippy's sources, he'd find out soon enough anyway. Besides, for all Rippy had done for Aaron, the least Aaron owed him was a truthful explanation. Aaron leaned forward toward Rippy and mumbled to prevent the surrounding customers from eavesdropping. "I've got a date, okay?"

Rippy started to laugh, then after his chuckle, he spoke. "Oh yeah, that's right, it must be that Campbell chick, the one that works down at the market. I've heard rumors about you two. Yeah that Campbell chick, the same chick I hear works part-time at Martin's topless bar." Rippy now looked cunningly at Aaron, who semi-lowered his head. "Yeah, that very same one. I guess there's nothing wrong with being an exotic dancer huh? I mean, it gets the bills paid."

Aaron was well aware of her other job; nevertheless, he didn't want his nose rubbed in it. With his present occupation, who was he to judge? "You can lay off that now, Rippy!" Aaron checked him.

"Okay, Smooth, okay, no need to get hot under the collar. But isn't that the same chick with that crippled kid?"

"He's handicapped due to his illnesses."

"Yeah, whatever. I heard his father left him some old valuable coins dating back to the Civil War. They're supposed to be priceless rare coins. Someone says he keeps it stashed under the bed ...."

Aaron charged, yanking Rippy by his coat. Customers looked on in surprise as Aaron held on tightly while Rippy tried unsuccessfully to pry loose from Aaron's hands.

The waitress signaled the cook, and he yelled to them both, "Hey, you guys, take that crap outside or I'll call the police!"

Rippy, now smiling, patted Aaron's shoulder. "We're okay, pal ... we were just kidding around."

"Well, if you have to kid, kid outside somewhere!" the cook growled.

Rippy attempted to coax Aaron to sit back down at the table.

"You listen here ...." Aaron was quick to caution, "business is business and I can separate it as being just that—business. But don't you ever go sticking your nose into my personal affairs ever again, do you hear me? You leave my personal life out of this—is that straight? You have that promise out of me toward your life without question. We do our business together, but after that, I don't meddle in your personal life. That's yours and your concern only—now do we understand each other?"

Still angrily focusing his eyes on Aaron as he plopped back into the chair, Rippy smiled and said, "Sure, Smooth. Why so hostile? I'm just saying how he had an expensive coin collection is all."

Aaron knew it was much more than just that, for he read into the ruse of subtle suggestion. Drinking the rest of his juice, he matched wills with Rippy in a stare down.

After a while, Rippy broke the silence, getting back to the specifics of their next job.

* * *

Midday, back at Big Motor City Market, business was moving at a snail's pace. Miss Beasley was shopping again and was in the household items aisle—detergents and pest sprays—after passing Audrey earlier saying she needed a few canned food goods. Audrey, foreseeing a potential catastrophe in the making, felt it best to commit herself to assisting Miss Beasley with her shopping for the greater good of her health.

This made for a perfect opportunity for the eager-eyed Kasam, with the aid of his manager's register key, to craftily swipe the fifty dollars from Audrey's register drawer. As Audrey continued helping Miss Beasley, they discussed a number of current events, high prices, and even how she hadn't seen her cat as of late.

As her shift came to an end, Audrey turned in her drawer as she customarily did. Tossing off her apron, she glanced at the clock above the coat rack, assuring herself that she had more than enough time to pick up her son's prescriptions. She impatiently watched the time clock so that she could punch her card, complete her errands, rush home to check on Devon, fix dinner, take a short nap, then get dressed and go to her second job. However, two minutes before the clock struck, signaling quitting time, she was paged by Kasam who was standing in the manager's booth.

Audrey held onto her punch card and thought, *Now of all times!* Kasam's was definitely the last face she wished to see at closing time. Her guard raised, she approached Kasam quietly, ready to counterpunch. He pointed to the rear office and said, "Azid wishes to speak to you."

She didn't have a clue as to why Azid had sent for her. *Could he be needing me to work more time?* she thought as she trotted in that direction. *Maybe I gotta check inventory again,* she wondered, feeling displeased at the very thought. However, she felt an omen of ill will descend when she sensed Kasam following right behind her.

She knocked at the door and Azid opened it. Immediately she realized that the omen she had sensed could not have been more correct, for Azid's entire disposition was odd; not once after she stepped foot through the door could he bear to look into her eyes. Audrey, unable to bear any more suspense, spoke her question directly to Azid as Kasam swiftly entered and closed the door behind him.

"Mr. Nadir, what's the problem? I haven't done anything wrong, have I?"

Azid's words were brief. "Kasam believes your cash drawer short of money."

Audrey, with a never more open display of innocence, opened her mouth in deep shock, but her voice was barely audible as she exclaimed, "What?"

Kasam jumped in, taking full command of the inquisition. "That is correct. You stole money out of the drawer! I've checked at end of day your cash receipts and money in drawer and it's short by sixty dollars!"

Audrey, directing her comment to Azid, said, "Mr. Nadir, there must be a mistake or an oversight. I'd never . . ."

"No mistake. I double checked. Sixty dollars out of your drawer gone! Taken only by no one but you!"

Audrey stood looking at Kasam and said, "Now that's a lie!" Looking over to Azid, she pleaded, "Mr. Nadir, believe me, this isn't true. I've worked here for two and a half years and never once has my drawer turned up a nickel short!"

Azid, shifting at his desk, grimaced with his hands covering his face.

Kasam, pulling cleverly from his backup, said, "You would deny a truth that is right here in front of you? What about other day when you undercharged woman on food bill? Would you deny that?"

Audrey, now turning around, asked, "Woman? What woman?"

"You would deny that too? When woman told me that you did, she played lottery at my station for man who brings good luck!"

Audrey remembered the incident and, not being gifted with a true poker face, couldn't hide the guilt that shone on her face. "Aha! You see there, it is true!" Kasam exclaimed, pointing his finger in her face for Azid to view.

Audrey whispered, feeling terrible, "I might've done that."

"You see, Azid, how quick she is to lie! She did take money from drawer as I have said! I shall call the police right now." Kasam began dialing as Azid looked uncomfortable watching him dial.

Audrey protested, depressing the phone receiver. "I said no! I did not take sixty dollars from my drawer. I didn't do it! It's around here somewhere. It just must've been misplaced."

"No. Have not been misplaced! You took it!"

"I've told you, Kasam, I did not! Mr. Nadir, I'll be right back. I'm going to check my apron and my cashier area."

Azid tiredly waved her on while she grabbed her purse, exiting the office. Kasam redialed the police. Audrey looked carefully around her workstation area and found nothing. Picking up her apron, she likewise found nothing. She drew a blank as to where the lost money could be. Looking about hopelessly, she saw both the manager and owner still busy in the rear office from the corner of her eye. Surreptitiously using her apron as a cloak, she pulled money from her purse and pants pockets, clearing the entire amount needed for Devon's prescription and all pocket money that she had, leaving her only with a single dollar bill and six cents in change. Realizing what she was doing, she closed her eyes tight in prayer, hoping her child could do without medication for just one night.

Tears rolled down her cheeks but she swiftly cleared them, then screamed out, "Mr. Nadir, I've found the money!" She rushed back into the office. "Mr. Nadir, I've found your money!" she said, as she dropped the crumpled up bills upon his table. They both looked on in awe, especially Kasam, who couldn't believe what he was seeing.

Kasam hung up the phone as silence filled the room. He gathered the money and said, "It . . .it makes no difference. You've short charged woman, so you're fired!" He left the room and headed to his office.

Audrey, after a moment of standing in silence, couldn't bring herself to look up to Azid. Two years of faithful service, and now, in less than ten minutes, it had all washed away. She slowly left to clear out her personal items from her workstation. Not a word did she speak to anyone as she calmly strolled out the door her final time.

It wasn't until she was half a block away that Azid called out to her, running towards her onto the street. She walked halfway to greet the old man.

He felt somewhat guilty—but didn't relay this to Audrey— and told her he couldn't fire her, so he documented her leaving as a signature of resignation. He hoped to bridge any resentment that she might have by personally recommending her name to one of his friends who owned a liquor store across town and needed a trusted cashier. She took the number out of courtesy but knew full well she couldn't accept the job as it was so far across town that she would never be able to take care of her son. Having eight more weeks left in her medical assistant training course, she figured she could possibly work four nights a week at Martin's bar rather than two.

The hours passed and the evening rolled by, and Robbie soon found himself scratching upon another door. After scratching for some time and getting no results, he caught himself, remembering to stand in the windowsill behind the television to block the view of the woman inside. Miss Beasley, catching a glimpse of him, excitedly rose up from her chair to open the door for her "cat."

"Where have you been, Thomas? I was just telling all my friends I believed something happened to you."

"If you only knew the half of it," Robbie thought.

As long as Robbie could remember, Miss Beasley had always believed he was a cat named Thomas. Her eyesight was plain and simply just that bad. Depending on what time of the month it was, if she could afford it she always provided a milk dish alongside of his meal bowl. His food dish was, in itself, a different story, for on each visit there was always a surprise potluck, so to speak. Sometimes Miss Beasley would luck out and buy cat food. Or some days, he was more than thankful when she accidentally slipped up and purchased cans of dog food. Other days, he'd mistakenly find cling peaches, canned turnip greens, peas, or chili in his food bowl. One day poor Miss Beasley, to his surprise, opened a can of Drano and left it in his dish.

"I know you're probably close to starved. Let me just reach into my pantry and find you a can of food."

Robbie took a brief look around and waited, hungry and watching, intensely hoping she'd made a correct selection, because in his present condition, he could have devoured even cat food as a delicacy. Wishing he could speed her along the way, he peeked around her to the inside of the pantry, hoping for the right selection. Miss Beasley constantly talked to him as if he still sat prone at the door. He looked carefully at her unsteady hand as it selected.

Oh no, not strained beets! he thought. Craftily he startled her by brushing against her, as she continued speaking as if he was still across the room. She jumped, then turned around to look down at me.

"Oh, mercy sakes, Thomas, you trying to scare the poor life out of me?" Still turned towards him, she absentmindedly reached for another can, and much to Robbie's pleasure, it was a can of hash. He could live with that.

Finishing the meal, he sat for a spell to hear her converse, then as customary payment—as he had always done—he went in no real hurry to search for his bounty. Coming across one, he lazily grabbed the tail end of a mouse caught in a trap, yanking until it released. Unintentionally taking a strong whiff, it watered his eyes.

Whoa, what a stinker! How long you been lying in that trap, fella?

Robbie displayed the dead mouse to Miss Beasley, and she hooted with glee. "Thomas, you've caught another one!" She opened the rear door as he discarded it, then he went snooping for another sprung trap.

Coming across another one, he paused for a second. *Oh boy! This one is bringing a pain to my nose. This one has begun separating in every which direction!*

Miss Beasley clapped again with excitement upon seeing his second catch. She opened the door again, then upon his quick reentry, she welcomed him with a thorough petting session. Afterwards, feeling a bit smug, he took a nap while she continued her backlogged conversation. Much later, Robbie awoke to Miss Beasley's snoring as she had fallen asleep in front of the television. He clobbered himself since he'd nearly overslept and forgot an important errand across town that he had to complete.

He first brushed against her with no effect as she snored, sleeping soundly. He then scratched at the door heavily, hoping it would jar her to consciousness. After even this failed, he used the more direct approach. She alarmingly jumped to the loud bark of a dog right in her left ear.

"What? What was that, Thomas?" She observed him scratching on the door. "Oh my. Thomas wants to go outside?"

Robbie couldn't wait for her to open the door as he broke out, jumping off the porch in full stride since he had to cover such a distance. Not once breaking his stride, he ran a mile or two through the late-night city streets; a car horn blew at him as he slid across the road. Seeing three-legged Johnny, he didn't have time to speak or catch up on the latest gossip. Scampering another quarter mile, he turned a corner and ran blindly, right smack-dab into the middle of his assured doom.

Uh-oh, it's trouble! He stood within the grasp of the feared Second Street Gang—a band of young adolescent ruffians who Robbie classified as delinquent man-children, always eagerly spouting their misguided egos at any target due to their raging hormones. However many times they'd crossed paths, Robbie was beginning to lose his patience with their excuses of temporary insanity at his expense. Robbie didn't backtrack fast enough, and one of the youths kicked him square in the ribs as another screamed at the top of his voice, "Get him!"

Attempting escape, Robbie was pelted with rocks and broken bottles exploded around him. Fleeing, panting deeply, he thought, *Some human kids. Shucks, who'd ever think of them growing up and having the mental capacity to construct flying machines, to wage war on each other, and destroy a world? Noooo, not from a charming and endearing lot as this bunch.*

The gang chased him inside a multi-level parking garage as their vehement shouts and insults struck an ominous chord of impending doom. .

The gang spread out on the first level and Robbie tried rather foolishly to slip between them, but he was repelled back and hit with a bottle with brilliant accuracy from quite a distance.

Ouch! Now that, kids, got an arm. I say—sign him up! Limping up to the second level, Robbie looked down upon the kids as one pointed at him and shouted, "Get that loser tramp!"

That may be altogether true for me, so now tell me, what's your mother's excuse? Robbie thought while tiredly looking at the boy. Robbie could sense that this situation had rapidly declined from bad to worse. He took a second to gather his thoughts and now had a strategic plan as to how to get out of the garage with his skin intact—if he was quick enough. He limped toward the third level.

The group scattered about on the dark second level, searching slowly, trying to find and eradicate what they considered a nagging pest. The leader, bunching his troops together along the overhanging side of the parking structure, was in the process of mapping out a plan to trap the mutt on the third level. Huddled together with their heads down, they felt a gentle pelting of warm liquid, which one member—having the IQ of a goldfish—misinterpreted as rain. The gang screamed in disgust as Robbie looked down upon them, admiring his handiwork.

Hmm, so they didn't care too much for my rendition of 'Raindrops Keep Fallin' on My Head,' eh? Settling into his hiding spot in the shadows of a darkened crevice amidst some pipes, he heard the profanity laden, all-out battle cry as the gang rushed like wild banshees up to the last level.

Well, as I said before, what'd you expect from an uncultured angry lot such as this?

As the gang spread out onto the third level, Robbie knew they would be driven and blinded by anger. He watched them approach, most still a distance from his spot, until one passed in front of him, wiping his face frantically—Robbie saw his chance to escape.

Breaking out of the darkness quickly, Robbie brushed right by him.

The youth yelled out.

Now running in the lead, Robbie looked back to see the kids tripping over each other, attempting to catch him. As he ran towards the entrance, he was surprised to see they had the smarts to leave a sentry. Before Robbie could even think, he ran right into the path of the waiting juvenile who eagerly held a gleaming pocketknife in his hands. It was all happening too fast. As Robbie quickly approached the sentry, he could see the wide arc of the blade. It was too late to react. All he could do was close his eyes, say a prayer, and duck.

Looking behind him, his feet still in full sprint, Robbie could see and sense that the reckless youth had missed his mark. Robbie continued running all-out, eyes forward and alert, not stopping until he was sure the disgruntled youth gang was lost in the distance.

Meanwhile at Martin's bar, Mr. Martin himself was closing up shop. Audrey, after gathering her outfits and storing them in her carry-on bag, asked him if there was any chance for more work. Mr. Martin was bussing a table, but took time out to speak.

"Sure, my darling, you can start next week during our first anniversary celebration; it's been a year now since I bought this closed-down pub from Tony. You know, Audrey, you're a good employee. I've had an eye on you, like with the rest of the employees, and you're a good girl. You don't cause any rifts and you don't flirt with the customers. I like that. So, if there's anything you need, just let Uncle Marty know and I'll see if I can fix it up. By the way, how's that son of yours?"

Audrey, sounding discouraged, answered, "He's been better. His health has failed him the past couple of days."

"Don't cha fret none, he'll get over it. From what people been telling me, he sounds like a real fighter. You hurry up home, 'cause I'm not going to pay you overtime for a chat."

Audrey had already called a cab, and as always felt an urgent need to depart from the bar as soon as possible so she could purge herself from the tight, cramped, smoke-filled interior and get out where she could breathe the fresh, breezy, outside air. Outside she felt as if she had cleansed herself of all the dirtiness inside. She walked further up the street, her mind consumed with ever-surmounting problems. A car exiting from the lot of the closed bar caught her attention as it pulled alongside her. Not really wanting to look in, she heard the familiar voice of the bartender asking if she needed a lift. Audrey didn't really trust this individual or the way he eyed the girls and refused the offer graciously.

"Okay. Don't say I didn't ask!" The car sped off, emitting a loud, cannon-like boom in its departure.

It wasn't until after the fumes from the car's busted exhaust cleared that she took time out to notice her situation. She was alone, late at night, on a poorly lit street.

Where is that cab? she thought. She turned, walking back toward the bar, but noticed the lights were already out and the door padlocked from the outside. Everyone, including Mr. Martin, was long gone. She was about to turn back toward the street when, she witnessed an individual who had been jolted awake sitting in the parking lot inside his car.

She had seen the intoxicated man earlier while dancing, and by Mr. Martin's orders, the bartender was directed to not sell him any more drinks. It was then that he had become belligerent and started shouting profanities at many of the dancers, causing the bouncer to toss him out of the place. Apparently he had found refuge in his car and had managed to sleep off part of his drunkenness, but judging from his reaction at seeing her face, it was quite clear what ungentlemanly thoughts he was leaning toward.

Audrey was concerned for her safety and picked up her pace as the man started his car and followed behind her slowly. Not wanting to trigger panic within herself or elicit a predator response within him by breaking into a run—where he would feel dominate and provoked to overpower his "prey"—she merely ignored him and his rude gestures.

In hindsight, Audrey wished she had accepted the bartender's offer, figuring she would have had a far better chance fending off his advances than being caught in this predicament. However, a ray of hope shined from across the street in the form of a phone booth.

Audrey took a sharp turn to cross the street and approached the well-lit phone station. Seeing that the opposite phone's entire front surface had been vandalized, she picked up the other phone receiver and tried everything within her power to keep her sanity upon discovering no dial tone. Keeping her cool as the man sat in the car watching from across the street, she placed money into the inoperable machine as her coins confirmed her fears and immediately fell, ringing to the bottom of the phone. From the corner of her eye, she watched the car swing a slow U-turn in front of her. She began speaking loudly into the phone. "Yes, police, I'm here. That's correct. Three blocks north of West Grand Boulevard."

The man, hearing this, exited his car and approached her. "No, tell them it's two blocks south of the boulevard on the 2300 block of McGraw."

Audrey talked even faster into the phone the closer he got. Then he stood right over her.

"Did you tell them your exact location?" The man spoke, holding up—to her dismay—a long severed phone cord that dangled from the end of the receiver.

To her bewilderment, she became frozen with fear. Her eyes then wandered up into the man's eyes; he looked at her with a sinister smile. Dropping her carry-on sack, she shoved with all her might and fled running as the man, close behind, yanked her. She let fly a vicious right and struck him on the side of the head. But he was of a sizeable build, and the hit didn't faze him as he embraced her closer. Turning her around as she screamed, he quickly covered her mouth. She could smell the rank, putrid odor of alcohol and cigarette smoke on his breath.

"You gonna do one last dance for me, baby?"

Audrey tried to move away but couldn't. Her leg dangled freely between his. She suddenly calmed down to prepare to implement, as her mother called it, the "reliable old bread-and-butter approach." Growing limp within his clutches, she looked more relaxed and stared deeply into his eyes.

He, in turn, smiled and relaxed his grip.

Audrey returned a smile with her eyes as her attacker gave a mild giggle. Then with all her might, she thrust her knee straight up. But the man, cleverly foreseeing this tactic, swiftly blocked the fast-approaching knee in its tracks, holding it still with his tremendous strength.

"Uh, uh, uh, uh, uhhhh. I've seen that move quite a few times before," he smiled.

She bit his hand that covered her mouth. He grunted, "I can see you're one of those who like it rough, huh?"

The man let out an abrupt scream as Robbie locked onto a mouthful of his calf. He tossed Audrey loose as he shook spastically, trying to release the dog.

Audrey, in tears and crying aloud, found a tree limb and crashed it upon her attacker's head, then lost all composure, spewing a nonstop flurry of swear words at him. She bashed him with the tree limb repeatedly, as he slowly crouched, heading downward with each blow like the head of a nail being rapped by a hammer. She hit him with such force that she broke the limb over his head and began jabbing him furiously with the broken stump.

The man, kicking aimlessly at Robbie, trying to get free of his gnarling fangs, wrenched the tree stub from Audrey and threw it at her, managing with what strength and sobriety surfaced to make it to his feet, run toward his car, and speed off into the night.

Audrey still stood, crying deeply and covering her face with her hands. She suddenly backed away from the concerned Robbie who was approaching her, while screaming, "No! You just stay away from me! Just keep away! This is all your fault! All your fault! If you would've been here when you're supposed to, this all would've never happened, never happened!" She cried hysterically, nearly losing her voice.

Robbie sensed something was terribly wrong as he looked at her anguished face.

"I shoulda known I could never trust you, never depend on you. You just up and left us—for no reason. You're a bum, a traitor, a coward. I hate you. I hate your very existence, you deceitful snake. You left us. Left us all alone, and I hate you."

Audrey sank down, sitting in the gutter of the street and blubbering uncontrollably as Robbie stood in amazement, staring from what he considered a safe distance. She began muttering to herself. This drove Robbie—against his better judgment—closer. As he inched ever so gingerly towards her, she wrapped her arms around her body, resembling a ball, and began to rock herself, gently mumbling, "My pledge, my pledge, I can't lose my pledge. I must hold onto my pledge. Nothing will take it away ever again, I promise. Nothing."

Robbie, feeling the need to guard her, sat closely nearby in the street, facing Audrey. After a while, as if in a trance, she arose and gathered her bag as if he wasn't even there. She began to walk the long journey home. Robbie, limping along three steps behind, escorted her, ensuring her safety.

A number of days had passed and Robbie was still avoiding the Campbell household. It was nighttime, and although he had received two handouts earlier, he still rummaged around in an alley for a morsel. He had visited Aaron, who had sensed that Robbie was pretty much standoffish and wanted nothing but a meal and a quick exit. Aaron obliged him after receiving a salty hello, but upon Robbie's exit, Aaron had informed him that he would be needed for their next job in a few days.

Robbie appeared unconcerned and glided nonchalantly down the stairs. Now inside the alley, he found a bite and chewed into the morsel with the burden of his life weighing heavily on his shoulders. He attempted to sort the ever-increasing problems into a reasonable order. Unexpectedly, he heard a soft familiar voice.

"Purrr-cisely my intentions. May I join you?"

"Swift Claw? Sure, ah, help yourself," Robbie said, surprised.

After eating a while, Robbie, unusually quieter than Swift Claw, finally mentioned, "Glad to see you made it out okay over at Derek's Steak and Lobster House."

"Oh, w-eerrre there any doubts?"

They sat in silence for nearly fifteen minutes as Swift Claw closed her eyes for a catnap. Robbie looked upon her curiously. "Swift Claw, have you ever loved?"

Her eyelids slowly opened and she peered directly into his eyes. She gave a full yawn, then blinked several times. "Humans? Naw."

"I mean, ever?"

She paused, then turned her head away from him. A few minutes later, she spoke. "Naw—I mean, never again. I mean . . . even I had a life once."

Robbie, sensing she felt quite uncomfortable, didn't pursue it. "I was once like you, Swift Claw—a loner—and it worked fine for me. I hadn't a need for anybody, no one depended on me. And it worked perfectly until . . . until then."

Shifting his thoughts, he continued. "You—out of all the friends I've ever had or ever known—you were the only one I felt knew where I was coming from. Us both being loners, I knew you would have some idea of what I'm feeling. I don't understand this love thing. And I don't like it. If it's supposed to be good for you, why does it hurt so bad, huh?"

Swift Claw, speaking as Robbie had never heard her speak before, said, "Once I was purrr-plexed with that disgusting disease called l-o-v-e. Until I finally rid myself of it, and then I was never happier. I know of your love. I, unlike you, never had a need for this love, nor trusted, a human." Swift Claw stood up to look beyond the alley into the street. "I'm a warrior. My life is lived with the ever-impending threat of death. That's why I have no problems in this life. My advice to you is to seek your path, accept it—then live it!"

Robbie's mind was clouded with deep thoughts, which spanned moments of silence, and then the clouds finally broke. "Swift Claw, I've just had a striking revelation! Please, if anything happens to me, you must promise me one simple thing."

Swift Claw, looking at him said, "Purrr-haps. I'm not known for purrr-forming requests."

"Please, all I ask of you is for you to visit Old Lady Beasley. You know her. Just please visit her now and then to protect her. Then I'd know she would be safe with you being a warrior and protector and all."

Swift Claw took a long time to answer, then spoke, "If it is to be your final request, it shall be purrr-served as an honor in your name, my friend."

* * *

Two days had elapsed. Sitting in a downtown restaurant, a couple had already ordered dinner, were halfway finished dining, and were now engaged in a mild discussion, which was predominately about Audrey—from her "untimely resignation" from the Big Motor City Market to her looking forward to completing her medical assistant training classes.

Audrey looked across the table at Aaron, who, during the whole course of the date, appeared cordial and polite and, through her talks of disillusioned doubts, had aptly expressed encouragement. She found his manners quite appealing. She felt that as a person, somehow he could fully understand what she'd been going through. She had even admired his dapper appearance on their date, yet she was indeed leery of him. Not once did he say anything about himself. Anything that she hinted at regarding his personal life was met with a quick yes or no answer, followed by a smile, and that was it. Finally, out of concern, she snuck a question upon him while he was drinking his beverage.

"So, Mr. Aaron Davis, what do you do for a living?"

She truly caught him off guard. Suddenly, his eyebrows arched back, and he choked on the beverage he was drinking, causing the backflow to embarrassingly pass through his nose. Grabbing his napkin, with tears springing from his eyes, he continued a deep-bellowed cough, trying to clear the beverage from the wrong pipe. He bent forward slightly, covering his mouth with the napkin. "Well, errr, ahem, I'm a mover. Move things from one place to the other, you know." He sipped a drink of water.

"So, with this job, do you travel a lot?"

"Ah, yeah, sometimes. More than I like."

Audrey, switching her stance, said, "You know, somehow I got this feeling you don't care too much for your job. You probably feel somehow trapped?"

Aaron, smiling and sipping his water again, lightly tapped his fingers daringly on the table looking for their waitress. "That's a very good description," he muttered, "and if I'm not quite careful, I could find myself spending the majority of my life being trapped behind that job."

Audrey, speaking in a lighter tone, asked, "Oh, so you're looking for a new career yourself, huh?"

Aaron overcame his grim thought and smiled. "Yeah, you could say that."

Audrey returned his smile as he offered dessert, but she declined. He signaled for the check and they left the restaurant. She tried showing interest and support by helping him explore various employment options, suggesting that with his college background, many technical fields might be open to him—some with added training, others without. He, having a sense of humor, stretched some of her suggestions in a jokingly manner and they exchanged laughter as they strolled through the misty rain on the downtown city streets.

* * *

While at the Campbell's apartment, Pamela Williams heard the sounds of a familiar scratching at the door. Walking swiftly to the door, she swung it open in surprise. "Well now, I don't know whether to kick you, hug you, or refuse to let you through the door."

Robbie ticked, gathering he had little time. "Since it's a multiple choice question, how about just shutting your trap and moving aside?" Skirting by her, he ran into Devon's room, leaping onto his bed and staring him directly in the face.

Pamela, watching now, spoke to herself, "I guess it's okay to leave you two alone."

Devon's sickly, tiny eyes opened slowly. From this and other quick assessments, Robbie perceived that his condition had declined dramatically. "Hey ya, kid, thought upon my return, I'd see you up and walking by now. Remember, you are going to walk. I promised one day, I'd live to see you walk."

184

Devon's eyes opened wider. "You ... you're not dead? Mom t-t-told me you-you were not ever coming back. You . . . you were dead."

"What? Me dead, kid?" Robbie opened his mouth, tilting his head sideways as his big floppy tongue dropped out, dangling to the side. "Naw. You know me and business. I've been busy is all. Haven't got much time though, so just in case, I came to say . . . in the event I might get tied up, you know, maybe for a very long, long time . . ." Suddenly, Robbie, found himself unable to look Into Devon's now hope-filled, inquisitive eyes. Closing his eyes temporarily, Robbie hoped it would shut the flow from his tear ducts. "I-I, just had to tell you, kid . . ."

Devon, with all his effort, touched Robbie's hairy belly under-coat. "I know, and I love you too."

Robbie collapsed on the bed in front of him and he turned his head away from Devon, hiding, refusing to be weakened by his tears.

With Robbie's brief few minutes before his departure, he whispered quietly, "You know, kid, people might say . . . upon my absence . . . that I might be dead again, but don't you believe it. No, 'cause just as sure as I'm with you now, I promise I'll still be by your side."

At that moment, back on the downtown city streets, Aaron and Audrey ran across at a now flashing yellow traffic light. Audrey laughed, trying to out sprint him across the street in the freezing rain. She caught an ice patch and slipped to the oppo-site sidewalk, tripping on the embankment and nearly falling, until Aaron guardedly caught her hand, preventing her from hit-ting the pavement. Amazed at the human spirit and how quickly shock can instantaneously turn to receptive compassion, she had already passed the barrier of holding his hand and was now in danger of shattering her pledge by looking the way she pres-ently did into his eyes.

The drums of caution banged loudly in protest now, as he slowly, gently, embraced her. Drawing her nearer toward his warmth, secure from outside forces. The pledge that she now held clinched in her hand had fractured, and the slowly moving cracks traveled end to end. There were suddenly only two people in the world; two people attempting to break beyond a harsh barrier—a barrier so unfair and overwhelmingly against them, that a time for true love in this day and age just didn't seem possible. Chivalry, courtship, compassion, and romance all seemed to be things in the city long since gone, but this day was a day of renewal. All things that once were, shall again come to be. One's hope, one's wish, another's love, shall come true today. Now the pledge that was once Audrey's had separated into a thousand pieces and blown mercilessly about in the chilling misty Detroit City wind. She was left embraced, staring, her lips within inches of Aaron's.

Aaron, now stumbling, attempted to speak. "There . . . there's something I feel I have to tell you be-before I kiss you."

"Okay." She reached closer.

A loud piercing air horn numbed their senses as Officer Raniette laughed with his finger on the horn button and Officer Price sat riding shotgun. Raniette kidding said, "Miss, this guy wasn't trying to assault you or anything, was he?"

He broke into a laugh as Price murmured to him to settle down.

"You know these two officers?" Audrey, looking surprised, questioned.

"Yes, old Darryl over there—we go way back from middle school. You could say he's got it in for me—in more ways than one. He still won't let me live down that open field tackle hit back in '74 that I gave him as linebacker for Mackenzie High in our senior year. He was wide receiver for Northwestern High. He was a grade A, recruited by colleges all around, and I snapped his ankle in two. He fumbled the ball, I picked it up, ran it back for a near touchdown, and he's never let me live it down since."

Price, grimacing from truth, as he could still vividly see that fateful day wallowing in the home team's mud, clutching his broken ankle and seeing his dreams of college and pro-football being dashed by one careless move to gain an extra yard. And Aaron was the one that orchestrated his dashed hopes.

Ranietti, becoming protective at seeing his partner become unglued, was about to speak in his defense, but was stopped as Price raised his hand. "That's okay, Aaron, old buddy of mine, just out of respect for your lady friend here, I just hope when the tables are turned and, this time you slip up, this lovely lady's hand will be there to catch you!"

Price now waved his hand forward and his partner sped off.

Aaron stood gridlocked, looking still at the disappearing path of the scout car long gone. Audrey, looking into his eyes, seemed lost. Aaron, nixing the thought, wrapped his arm around her, smiling, as they continued journeying through the downtown streets on their way to see a late movie, as a light snow began to fall.

* * *

Thirty-four hours passed. Just past midnight, about three inches of snow had continuously fallen. A dog appeared at the front gate of the Renaissance Technical Designs Partnership building. Robbie sniffed at the front gate as an electronic camera followed him. He began to walk a slow circle around the building as the cameras trailed him. Two men dressed in dark clothing and ski masks snipped the barbwire fence with ease, then ran undetected behind the view of the cameras using Robbie as a decoy.

With a carefully rehearsed procedure, performed time after time, Aaron quickly nullified the window shock alarm, giving the go ahead. Rippy shattered it with a rubber-enforced metal object. At the sight of a passing car's beams, they both cautiously ducked behind the bushes that lined the front of the business. Hearing the car moving away, they both slithered quickly through the window. Aaron was quick to flash his new fangled, red bulb, penlight as Rippy, displayed the blueprint that mapped out their direction and particular choice of items sought. Traversing the dimly lit hallways, they were careful of their every step. Now coming to a clearing where there was a security camera, Aaron affixed one of his bicycle mirrors propped up with a bendable clothes hanger wire.

"Stay put and cover for me while I climb up to attach this to the lens," he advised. Scaling the columns using the intricately curved molding, he whispered, "Success."

Climbing back down, they scampered across the wide length of the warehouse, running toward a lighted room. Rippy, broaching the door first, reached out when Aaron stopping him from touching the door, checked it cautiously, looking carefully from a distance and seeing the door wasn't electronically bridged at all angles, he cautioned Rippy, "Each door may possibly be joined by a synapse connector, silent or audible. Whatever you do, don't touch a door or jostle the handle. A good breeze could trigger this system easy."

After opening the door, they crept beyond the confines of another corridor. Rippy eagerly pointed out a room matching it on the map, which read 'Central File Office.' Aaron now steadily working, hoping to disarm the alarm before jimmying the lock, felt this operation was going over the safe margin of time normally allotted. After moments of painstaking diligence, the alarm was disarmed, the door opened, and both men were plunged headlong into the needed files and disks. After a while of retrieving the designated files and discs, Rippy set out on his own, asking Aaron to gather the rest and tossing him the list.

Aaron wished he could make Rippy refrain from his wandering altogether, but knew an argument would ensue and only waste more valuable time. "Don't touch a thing!" he cautioned.

"Yeah, yeah," Rippy replied.

Aaron knew that burglary, as complex as it was to plan and put into practice, was basically a simple principle of mathematics on paper. The greater amount of time stacked up attempting to pull a caper in progress was inversely proportional to your odds of getting away. The ratio of being detected in this complex equation had never been a factor of concern for Aaron. Detection for him was a lesser constant, which comes into play only after the getaway or under one of two distinct possibilities: 1) the person involved is really ignorant about what he's doing or, 2) he simply has a desire to be caught.

It was doubtful Aaron realized just how right he was. With his back to an exiting Rippy, he didn't know how the mere action of Rippy pulling the door silently closed behind him upon his departure had just exponentially increased that lesser constant ratio of detection—which Aaron normally considered negligible—by about a hundred fold. As Rippy closed the door, realigning it to its connector, the silent alarm rang directly to the private alarm company. Within seconds, the alarm company patched into the police department, which in turn dispatched a patrol car. Unknown to the conspirators, within moments the car was en route.

Rippy came back and reopened the door, setting the alarm off again. "Man, you should see the stuff they got in this place. It's unbelievable. We'll have to hit this dump again!"

Aaron, turning around, asked, "Did you touch anything?"

"Course not. What do I look like, a dummy? You through there or what? We still got a coupla more items to snag."

"Just these last two."

After a few seconds elapsed, Aaron said, "Let's go!"

Aaron exited first. As he watched Rippy following behind about to close the door, he exclaimed, "Hey, idiot! Don't close that door! Leave it open. You want to reconnect the switches so the alarm will sound?"

Aaron started down the corridor as Rippy stared guiltily at the door.

Outside at the rear, Robbie rose carefully, observing two cars approach with their headlights off. He commenced barking a warning signal. Aaron slowed down to listen. "Wait, was that Robbie?"

"I didn't hear nothing."

A scout car pulled up along the front of the building. Ranietti and Price hopped out, fresh on their first tour of midnights. Exiting from a station wagon was a Mr. Blass.

Ranietti, shaking the hand of the gentleman dressed in a khaki jump suit, said, "The department appreciates you bringing your dogs out for a demonstration, Mr. Blass."

"Really, Officer, it's my pleasure to assist in any way possible for the prevention of crime, and please remember I supply the most state-of-the-art police equipment in the country. I simply wish your department would take a firm look at my canine security obedience school. It's the best canine school in the country!"

Robbie, sitting at his post, was stumped seeing this unusual sight. He did indeed notice one thing—the dogs being led out of the station wagon weren't city police dogs. With his experience, he knew the looks of the police dogs, and having had a close, chance meeting with them, he knew to be wary. He would never forget the encounter he had with an oversized bloodhound of theirs. Yet, these dogs were even more hardnosed, sharply tempered, and disciplined. Accessing the situation, Robbie thought that in his, Aaron's, and Rippy's best interest they needed to be out of there now! He sounded another flurry of warning barks that Aaron definitely heard this time, which caused him to freeze in his tracks.

"Let's go, quickly! We gotta get outta here!" he said with urgency.

"Hey, what's that?" Ranietti said, startled.

"It's him. I knew it would be him!" Price exclaimed.

"Mr. Blass, have your dogs fetch that mutt while we corner my old pal Smooth and his partner Rippy."

The dog instructor complied with a simple instruction. "Fetch!"

The dogs ran off in Robbie's direction.

Uh-oh, this has the makings of a very bad scene! Robbie thought, as he began fleeing in the opposite direction, still desperately barking continuous warnings to the occupants inside the building.

"Rippy, man, we have to cut this thing loose! Something's gone wrong!"

"Don't sweat it. He's probably bumped into some old playmates of his and is running around with 'em, the no good mutt, when he should be at his post."

Robbie ran heatedly, but the dogs quickly closed the distance. One of them snatched his dangling tail, causing his constant flurry of warning yelps to turn into a yip. All things considered, Robbie was grateful he knew of this tactic—one holds the tail while the others rip the dog to shreds. While the one held him still, another ripped at his side. He, in turn, attacked one, charging at his throat. With a quick move, he twisted to the ground, taking two along with him. The other dog viciously nipped at his exposed chest. Then with a twist of added strength, Robbie swung around, breaking loose from their grip, and climbed quickly to his feet, He made a dash again to get away.

Aaron and Rippy, attempting to cloak themselves, scaled the metal beams inside the warehouse and were now sitting atop the beams. They were startled when they found themselves staring down upon two searching flashlights below, while the sound of battling canines echoed from outside.

"You stubborn idiot! I told you he was trying to warn us about something!"

Rippy knew that the warning, since they hadn't heeded it, had now vaporized into nothingness. A different concern now arose in his head, for he was already a three timer, caught and convicted, and presently on parole. If he was captured again, his parole agent told him he'd be looking at ten to twenty minimum in Jackson State Penitentiary, with not even a hint at parole. The cards were definitely stacked against him, but he was determined by hook or by crook that there was absolutely no way he was going back to prison. Definitely no way was he going to be taken—by anybody.

Unnoticed by Aaron, Rippy reached underneath his shirt quickly and slipped the .25 caliber automatic handgun from his pants, concealing it behind his back.

Outside, the dogs had cornered Robbie again. They pasted him some good licks. He was breathing hard but stood defiant, awaiting the four standing in unison, gearing up for their next synchronized attack. He realized his only alternative was to bust through them or die.

"I'm beaten up pretty good." Robbie thought, feeling shock from the severity of his wounds and knowing he could never run fast enough to outrun them. But one thing he knew he was good for, and that was being the master of escape. He knew his best means of escape was rushing through one of them, and the best way to break a chain, as everyone knows, is through its weakest link. And this chain's weakest link was the dog he had viciously attacked at the throat earlier.

It's gotta be unexpected, he thought, panting hard and nearly out of breath from exhaustion and fear. *Wait!* He thought for a second. Looking beyond the dogs, he recognized his location— Rogue's Alley! He watched as the team apparently regained their bearings and prepared to move in. Robbie, cleverly playing the hurt and weakened possum, suddenly charged at the unsuspecting dog that had yielded who now backed away in a defensive posture. It was room enough to scamper by in a furious run. Now having a nice-sized lead, he ran through several vacant lots, attempting to shake off the hard noses as he headed towards Rogue's Alley.

I know Sharkey and the gang ought to be around to play with this eager bunch. Coming to the crest of Rogue's Alley, he yelled out in trouble, "Sharkey, Riptoe, Snaggletooth, Overbite, Lockjaw, Sasquatch—where are you?"

One of the hard noses tripped him up, and the four dogs were viciously on top of him, tearing away at will. Try as he might to feign off the onslaught, he was too weak from trauma, and

Robbie failed miserably in his feeble attempts to defend himself. Within seconds, it would all be over.

A sudden rustle from behind the dogs caught two of the team's attention. Now the aforementioned dogs and many others stood in a bunch, circling the group as they witnessed something they couldn't believe to be true.

"Hey, hey, hey now, hey now, hey now! What's this? These lugs be at our bro? We can't be having that, not here, not now!" Sharkey spoke. The other two dogs ceased their attack to see the small army.

"Oh no, now you fellas know what time it is! No one jumps my boy, Robbie, and comes away unscathed!" Snaggletooth beamed.

Riptoe, who only spoke in his usual patented four words, said, "I wanna kick butts!"

Huge Sasquatch, brandishing his larger-than-life fangs, led the charge as the group converged on the confused four. Robbie lay badly hurt, beaten and helpless. He was miraculously still breathing, yet unconscious.

* * *

Still attempting to escape from the warehouse, Rippy and Aaron watched as the search continued.

"They've caught us unless they enter that corridor and we make a dash for it!" Aaron whispered, still observing their closing approach. "You hear me, Rippy?"

Looking over to Rippy, into the dark and unable to see anything, Aaron ducked from sight as Ranietti surprisingly shone his light and locked onto a now visible Rippy, who had his .25 caliber automatic out, aimed directly at the exposed head of Officer Price, who walked below unsuspectingly.

"Are you insane? What are you doing?"

"Will you shut up? I ain't going back to prison!"

Instinctually, Aaron grabbed the gun and shouted, "Darryl, run! He's got a gun!"

Rippy fired two shots as Price dove beneath a forklift.

Rippy screamed at Aaron hysterically, "So you've gone soft on me! You've turned snitch, huh?"

Rippy aimed the gun at Aaron as they tussled with it. Three shots discharged as they continued fighting for possession of the gun. Ranietti, in his excitement, fired four shots at the struggling men. They both fell over each other, knocking down metal canisters. Aaron rolled over, near unconscious, while Rippy got up, running for an exit. Ranietti fired two more shots at him, then aimed his gun at Aaron.

"Don't shoot him! Don't shoot!" Price yelled.

Ranietti rushed forward and placed cuffs on him, then ran after Rippy as he radioed for back up.

"You okay? You're not hit, are you?" Price asked.

Aaron looked up, being placed on his stomach handcuffed from behind, and replied, "No, but I think my arm is broke." Aaron, thoroughly disgusted over this whole snafu, lamented, "Looks like I fumbled the ball this time."

"No, Aaron, you've made a great save—my life—and I thank you, pal!" Price said and then turned to join Ranietti in the chase.

Later, through information over their radio, the officers heard that another unit had successfully caught Rippy. Night passed and it was midday the next day. Robbie still lay in Rogue's Alley convalescing near the site where he was attacked. The Rogue's gang cared for him while he attempted to heal and regain some strength.

Two days passed as Aaron stood in lockup. Due to Rippy's accusations of him being a "yellow snitch," the detention officers put him into a solitary cell for his own safety. The prosecutor and defense attorney, both hearing about how Aaron had saved a policeman's life, worked to get the charges dropped to one count of entering without the owner's permission. This was dependent upon the business agreeing and the attorney understanding that Aaron would testify against Rippy on behalf of the prosecution.

Aaron agreed, feeling angry that Rippy tried to murder him. He felt Rippy should consider himself lucky that Aaron was not pursuing murder charges against Rippy too.

* * *

Another day passed, and a lawyer, vouching for his appearance, agreed to release Aaron on a personal bond, pending trial. However, the coming news Aaron was about to receive would leave him with big doubts about the security of the justice system.

Darryl Price was the first to alarm him. Apparently, just two hours before Aaron signed out, Rippy had gotten out of jail on a $100,000 dollar bond.

"Through his lawyer, Rippy wrote out a $10,000 dollar check," Price told him. "If you need me to watch over you, I can put you up. That's the least I can do!"

Aaron was crushed. He looked distant, gathering his thoughts about the possibility of what was to happen next. He just had to figure out what he was going to do.

"No. What I do now, I know I'll have to do alone. This is just between him and me." Aaron rushed out, and even before exiting the precinct door, he'd already figured Rippy's first move.

Meanwhile, Robbie made his first efforts at actually walking around and still convalesced in shards of pain at Rogue's Alley.

* * *

Inside the office of Dr. Val Larsons, things were slowly winding down as she switched off the last light in the business, the lamp over her desk. Lugging her oversized purse, which appeared to be loaded with half of everything under the sun, she remembered something. She reached deep down into her

bag to enjoy the apple she hadn't had time to eat earlier—
a just reward at the end of a hard day. Closing the door to
her office, the apple hampered her as she fumbled with her
keys while trying to lock the outer doors. Suddenly, her office
phone rang, and the answering machine proceeded to give the
caller a message: "You have reached Dr. Val Larsons's office in
the Center for Alternative Medicine. Presently, I'm away from
the office. If a medical emergency arises, please go to your
closest twenty-four-hour medical emergency facility. Thank
you—beeeeep."

An elated voice transmitted over the line. "Dr. Larsons,
it's incredible! It's Christmas in March—the response! This is
Dr. Stephen Berkiwitcz. Whatever you do, please . . ."

* * *

It was afternoon as Aaron unwrapped his broken arm from
the sling. Getting a cup of coffee at the corner restaurant just
across from Audrey's apartment building, he watched carefully;
he had been in hiding near Audrey's since his release from jail.
He hadn't seen his buddy Robbie for quite some time, and he
feared the worst had happened to him. Yet he couldn't mourn
his friend just now; he had to see this business through first.
Sitting patiently in the coffee shop, assuming Rippy would strike
at night, he was shocked to see the thief climbing to Devon's
window in the light of day—at that very moment! Dropping his
cup of coffee, he ran over to the apartment, taking the stairs
three at a time.

* * *

Toby mischievously sat at the end of the street corner,
eagerly trying to determine his choice of prey—which late
model car to commence his chase—and looked curiously at the
unusual sight before him. A strange man stood peeping inside of

196

Robbie's family's window. Toby ran, abandoning his childish game, and headed for Rogue's Alley where Robbie was held up.

* * *

Rippy opened the locked window with ease, then slipped in. Looking around, he was amazed by the various machines surrounding the small child. He pulled a knife out and crept toward the sleeping child. "Hey, sleepyhead. Yo, you freak, wake up!"

Devon's eyes opened to see a strange man standing over him dangling a knife while he lay helpless in his bed. "That can of valuable coins better be under this bed or you're going to be introduced to my brand of assisted suicide!"

* * *

At Rogue's Alley, Nephertiti stood over a still-recuperating Robbie while he spoke to her with a surprisingly ray of optimism. She listened with a sense of inspiration to his newly adopted life philosophy.

"You were right, Teetee, I had been neglecting my responsibilities, and I've seen the error of my ways. Swift Claw told me I should choose a path and live it. Well, starting today, I'm going to change."

Toby, out of breath, blazed a trail as he rounded the corner of Rogue's Alley. Seeing Nephertiti standing above Robbie, he blurted out, "Robbie, come quick! It looks like Devon's in deep trouble!"

Robbie immediately got up on all fours, ignoring the flashes of pain, and he dashed away without need of any other explanation.

* * *

Rippy carefully reached underneath the bed to claim his prize. Hearing the bedroom door swing open, he pulled out and leveled his gun at the doorway. Aaron stood in the doorway as Audrey peeped from behind him and screamed in terror, seeing the man standing next to her son's bed impaling the mattress with a knife.

"Well, it's the lovebirds and their happy family—or is it stool pigeon, snitch, former drug courier, or B and E man? Which one is it, Smooth? Have you told the pretty lady yet?"

"Rippy, you've been bad news since day one . . ."

"And I've made you. I've made you what you are today. You were nothing but a homeless lowlife bum until—"

Rippy put down the jar and pulled the knife out from the mattress as Audrey pleaded, "Please don't hurt my baby, sir, please!"

Aaron, stepping forward, said, "Come on, Rippy, this is personal, just between you and me. Nobody else is in this. Let's settle it outside, right now!

Rippy now turned his attention to the dialysis machine. "I know this; it's a kidney machine. Very expensive. Lots of money. This'll bring me a bundle of money on the market." He used his knife to cut the cord.

Audrey screamed and Devon looked scared seeing the knife slice through the wire. Aaron jumped at him. Rippy expected this as he countered and side-stepped, then fired three shots. One hit Aaron in the thigh, and he fell to the ground. Audrey ran screaming in panic, shouting for Miss Ford to dial the police.

Rippy dropped the knife, forced the can of coins into his pocket, wrapping the severed cord around the machine, prepared to carry it out. Devon nearly froze with shock as the machine ground to a dead halt, His mouth transfixed and open, and he looked as if he wanted to cry.

Like a bolt of lightning, Robbie leapt into the air and onto Rippy, attacking him with the unrestrained viciousness of a kill. With Robbie all over him, Rippy wildly fired two more shots and bailed out the window. Robbie, watching the fleeing man from the window, dashed out the bedroom door and ferociously charged through the hallway, bypassing a lost-for-words Mr. Honeycutt.

Aaron quickly grabbing the knife crawled to the dialysis machine's severed cord and with blind luck speedily reattached the cord. Plugging the machine in, he watched Devon's slow recovery. Audrey rushed back in, and seeing the cord reattached, she helped Aaron onto a chair.

"I'm okay," he grimaced. "Gotta help Robbie. He needs me!"

Audrey cautioned, "You're bleeding badly. He might've hit an artery. We've got to stop the bleeding!"

Robbie, anger-driven by Rippy's act of attempted murder committed toward his master, rounded the corner of the apartment and was running on full adrenaline as he saw Rippy escaping in the distance. Nephertiti and Toby likewise gave chase but backed off after Rippy fired gunshots directly at them.

Rippy crossed a street, ran between houses, and hurriedly pushed himself under duress to escape across a busy intersection during rush hour traffic. Robbie gained some ground when Rippy was forced to wait to cross over to the first half of the intersection. Boldly, fueled by adrenaline, Robbie pressed onward without hesitation. Then, from out of nowhere, a car smashed into him with tremendous force, sending him spinning end over end as if in slow motion, over the car and onto the hood, sprawling him onto the trunk, finally sliding him onto the hard concrete. Lying there for a second, he crawled a few inches, feeling that Rippy was still within his grasp—then he collapsed.

That's funny, he thought. *The ground was bone dry just a minute ago. Why is it wet under me now?*

Rippy, looking at what he thought was a hilarious sight, laughed aloud. "I guess that ends our partnership, eh?" he jeered.

He failed to pay attention and stepped just wide of his mark, inadvertently crossing into the path of a fast-moving bus that attempted to beat the oncoming red light. The sound of the collision was similar to a porterhouse steak being taken from the pack right out of the refrigerator and dropped from a measurable height onto a marble floor. Rippy's body now resembled a bug splattered on the windshield of an automobile that was doing seventy miles per hour on a freeway.

Robbie's attention was briefly taken by a coin that was rolling towards him. It lost its momentum and toppled in a whirl in front of his nose. Robbie amazingly couldn't feel any pain. He couldn't discern whether all his nerve fibers were detached from earlier, because he suffered so much pain, or if he was still on that adrenaline high. He only knew that he overwhelmingly desired a breath of air or a cool drink of water right now. He was unusually thirsty. Since he couldn't move his head, and all traffic had stopped, he figured he'd just lay there for a moment, like at Rogue's Alley, then he'd get up and walk back to the apartment to check on Devon—now that Rippy had gotten his just desserts.

"Ohhhhh!" he moaned, now feeling a twinge of discomfort as something in him felt like it gave way. He looked out of the corner of his eye and saw what resembled a white stick sticking out of his chest cavity. *Ha! Who do you suppose put that silly stick there?* he wondered. His field of vision was becoming clouded, and everything appeared as though he was seeing it through a long, distant tunnel. Feeling another twinge of pain, he surprisingly felt a sensation he hadn't felt—but had longed for—for some time now. It was someone rubbing his fur coat. His eyes moved upward. *Whoa, it's Mr. Honeycutt—I gotta get outta here!*

But then remarkably, and even stranger, he realized it was Honeycutt who was rubbing him. Honeycutt lingered momentarily, then stood up and backed away.

Robbie now felt the deep, hollow thump of his heartbeat tremor inside of him as it slowed to a crawl. *Okay, so who turned on that slow motion machine?*

Standing above him, he recognized as Dr. Larsons. *Oh no, every time I see this human, I get jabbed by needles.*

She stepped back.

Suddenly he felt himself growing numb. *Ohhh, oh-h. What's happening here? This is strange!*

Robbie felt a brush of cold arctic wind that froze his entire body. An instantaneous flash of a brilliant light startled him, and he felt himself being lifted beyond his control. Weightless, he had detached, watching himself tear away from his outstretched body lying on the pavement; he now remarkably hovered momentarily over his body. On the parking lane, he saw his buddies, Nephertiti and Toby, watching and grieving over their fallen friend. Gently he began to rise softly upon the soothing tranquil breezes of the air current.

"Hey look, gang. I'm flying! Look!"

He was breathless, and with a whoosh of a sweetly fragranced wind, he glided into a vacuum, slowly accelerating, traveling ever upward.

Suddenly, Devon's life signs mysteriously jarred, and the various machines flickered their warning lights. Aaron, without explanation, fell from his chair, catching himself as he felt helplessly incapacitated, as if someone had accidentally tripped an electrical plug to his entire body.

Robbie laughed as he glided steadily upward, passing through an alarmed flock of birds. Swift Claw's attention suddenly turned from an open garbage can as she, for some unforeseen reason, stared curiously into the seemingly vacant sky.

Robbie's speed increased as he breezed through the mist of clouds and thin-aired outer atmosphere. Traveling still further, he turned his body around in a dance of delight as he approached the dark space. He watched closely as fast-moving planets jetted beyond his presence, while his speed increased to astronomical proportions. He watched as billions of stars zoomed by; the acceleration was so enormous that the light from the stars became one. So fantastic was the speed and illumination from the light, so mesmerizing and so euphoric, that he yielded, closing his eyes, until finally he stood upon a doorstep—a doorstep leading toward a bright, truly incredible, enormous light of infinite dimensions.

* * *

As time passed, under the watchful eye of Nephertiti, Toby permanently gave up car chasing. In hindsight, he couldn't help but agree, like Robbie had told him countless times before, that the pastime was too reckless—besides being outdated.

Through the pioneering insight of Dr. Val Larsons, and the diligent footwork of Dr. Stephen Berkiwitcz in bringing the union of Doctors Saunders, Voltheim, and many others throughout the medical community together, the intricate operation took place. Robbie's bone marrow was transplanted into Devon The procedure took days and caught tremendous flak from many skeptics who questioned the specifics and resources of such an unorthodox surgery. However, upon occasion, miracles happen. The transplant surgery was a success, creating an ongoing working relationship between Dr. Larsons and Dr. Berkiwitcz.

In a year's time, as Robbie predicted, Devon did indeed walk. Robbie looked in on him from above, one final time, with great pride.

Swift Claw, true to her word, visited Miss Beasley from time to time. And Miss Beasley still bragged about her "cat." Swift Claw, in what could be described as her brand of affection, kind of grew fond of the offbeat Miss Beasley. She realized that, even if only embodied in just this one human, there were a few redeemable qualities somewhere within the deplorable human species.

Audrey's steel embrace of her perpetual pledge had been unconditionally abandoned on that first date with Aaron. Aaron, now believing in himself again, found this love an opportunity to try once more, and he enrolled in and completed courses in masonry and bricklaying. Audrey later became a medical assistant, and through chance, as in life itself, decided to give herself to love for one more try.

Robbie's "gang of family" still held their family dinner excursions from time to time. And since Robbie's departure, in his honor, the group would officially invite a drifter or stray into their family gathering.

Epilogue

Across the timeless boundary known as Heaven, twinkling with mesmerizing peace, a euphoric glee was quintessentially felt amidst its interior. All inhabitants were joyous in song, praise, and spirit. All save one. It was the tiny angel, Brian, who stood off isolated in a distant corner. Saddened with grief by the tales of the dogs, he somehow felt a sense of defeat.

He had not experienced this feeling since his initial discovery of his abrupt passing, prior to arriving here himself before these celestial walls. Sitting on a stoop, pouting, with his right hand clasping his frayed Teddy Bear. Looking upon the seemingly saddened eyes of the bear, he observed that the poorly stitched teddy had a rip in its seams and now leaked a mysterious slow gas, forming a shape before his eyes. And then the voice spoke.

"What troubles my wise angel?"

Brian looked on, as the gas repaired the stitch and then inhabited the bear, animating it. The bear stood, twirled around, took a bow, and climbed into Brian's lap. Brian looked sadly into its missing eye, and it repaired itself as he spoke.

"Brisk, Helena, Deake, Ramrod, 11736, Robbie."

"My little one, why worry so much? No matter how untimely precious innocent lives are taken, do not cry for them, for like you, they all answered the Lord's call bravely and shall thrive within my kingdom, knowing true love, peace, and acceptance."

As the whole plane lit up and radiated with brilliancy, the Lord spoke. "My creatures step into the glow of my glory. It is on behalf of you, my blessed souls, who gifted the world with courage, sacrifice, companionship, loyalty, and love. Stand now before me, my champions—reward us with your presence. Forever shall there be man, and there shall always be you."

Now appearing before Brian eyes, standing just as bold and as lively as they'd ever been, were the Lord's "champions."

Brisk stood at stark attention with authority. He bravely posed, determined to meet any challenge with the confidence and true heart of a fighter.

Helena and Deake, still inseparable, snuggled together in romantic bliss, both talented and unsurpassed in crime-solving intelligence and deductive reasoning. Helena, in courageous splendor, spanned a new age in crime detection, efficiency, and ingenuity. Deake, wise and experienced, was an icon of old-fashioned smarts, diligence, and patience.

Ramrod, posed sleek and agile, exuded confidence with the superiority of speed, as if ready to break out of the gates any second; he was truly a leader of unselfish altruism with unwavering integrity and a dedicated spirit.

Next, 11736 was in pristine health and stood before him, beaming unwavering courage of steel, a founding pioneer in his own right, possessing the valor within to explore. Bowing, without concern for self, his unbridled and unselfish loyalty in the ultimate sacrifice for the betterment of all was his crowning glory.

Robbie sat upright, his compelling, heartfelt, lovable, comedic gaze strong and warm—as always, with his tongue drooping over to the side, an example of dependable love, devoted responsibility, and lifelong companionship. He was still the scrappy, lovable, happy-go-lucky companion who brought luck and love to all who happened into his presence. During life's periods of trouble, he emerged as the catalyst that boosted new life in whatever heart he touched.

Brian stood within their presence, enjoying their treasured company.

"That's right my faithful ones, shine brightly. For their lives as dogs shall ever warm our hearts. Through this time, and time after time, may the spirit of goodness forever be!"

About the Author

Storyteller and dreamer, Irvin L. Cannon, put pen to paper for the first time in response to a challenge. A simple challenge issued in response to his comment... "I can write a better story than that." The challenge uttered, "Do it then!" He began scribbling story after story into notebooks now stored all over the house. *For the Love of Dog Tales* is the first release from those tucked away pages birthed from that short exchange.

Born and raised on the East Coast in large metropolitan cities, the author's fascination with storytelling began in his youth. His vision and imagination for the art of storytelling was primarily nurtured by his love for comic books. A scientist by training, dog lover by nature, and a man with many years in law enforcement, author Cannon's experience in the inner city street wars, combine to produce a biting view of the world around us as seen through the eyes of his canine characters—characters with whom he has crossed paths.

Cannon has seen and felt many atrocities imposed upon humanity and dogs in the performance of his duties. He has given the reader a window into the depth of emotions and cruelty experienced by the dogs, evidenced by their physical condition and the stories told through their eyes. *For the Love of Dog Tales* melds his love for a well-told story with his life experiences and love for animals.

The author presently resides in the Midwest with his wife.

Visit *Irvin Cannon's* website for:

Live Appearance Schedules
Contests and Giveaways
Promotions
Book Club Discounts
Helpful Links
Featured Organizations
Opportunities to Get Involved
New Projects

www.ILCannon.com

Expand your Influence, Share your Love, Network in the Global *For the Love of Dog Tales* Community. Get Connected to the *For the Love of Dog Tales* Global Community. Join for FREE

Just For Registering You Will Enjoy:

Inspiring Discussion Forums
Valuable Exchange of Ideas and Information
Exclusive Access to Special Offers
Appearance Notifications
Event Invitations
Insider Look at the Next Volume of the Series
And More

For the Love of Dog Tales is committed to communicating with you, providing valuable information and exciting opportunities. Follow the threads on Twitter, connect and participate in Facebook commentary and enjoy the benefits of Community Membership.

www.FortheLoveofDogTales.com

Made in the USA
Charleston, SC
04 January 2012